Also by Louis Sachar

Dogs Don't Tell Jokes

LOUIS SACHAR

Alfred A. Knopf • New York

THIS IS A BORZOI BOOK
PUBLISHED BY ALFRED A. KNOPF, INC.

Text copyright © 1991 by Louis Sachar
Jacket art copyright © 1991 by Jim Warren

Library of Congress Cataloging-in-Publication Data
Sachar, Louis, 1954–
Dogs don't tell jokes / by Louis Sachar. p. cm.
Summary: Twelve-year-old Gary, known as Goon because of his
constant clowning and joke-telling, tries to change his image and
make new friends at school.
ISBN 0-679-82017-5 (trade) — ISBN 0-679-92017-X (lib. bdg.)
[1. Self-perception—Fiction. 2. Schools—Fiction.] I. Title.
PZ7.S1185Do 1991 [Fic]—dc20   91-2042

Manufactured in the United States of America

2 4 6 8 0 9 7 5 3

To Ace

I meant what I said
And I said what I meant....
An elephant's faithful
One hundred per cent!

—Dr. Seuss, *Horton Hatches the Egg*

Dogs Don't Tell Jokes

1.

This story begins with a smile.

⏝

It was a stupid-looking smile on a rather stupid-looking face. Maybe it was the smile that made the face look stupid. Or maybe it was the face that made the smile look stupid. It was difficult to tell because the two were rarely apart.

It was the smile on the face of Gary Boone.

He was in the seventh grade at Floyd Hicks Junior High School. Just about everybody there thought he was a goon. They called him Goon right to his smiling face.

"You're an idiot, Goon, you know that?" Paul Wattenburg said to him one morning.

"No, as a matter of fact I didn't," Goon said, then laughed.

He called himself Goon too. On the first day of school, his math teacher, Miss Langley, asked him his name and he said, "Goon."

"I beg your pardon," said Miss Langley.

"See, my name's Gary Boone," Gary explained, "so you take the G from Gary and the 'oon' from Boone, and you put them together and get 'Goon.' Ha. Ha."

Miss Langley went on to something else.

Last year at the end of sixth grade, Gary was voted Class Clown. He took it as a great compliment. He wanted to be a stand-up comic when he grew up. "Or a sit-down comic," he would sometimes say, "if my legs get tired."

Unfortunately, however, nobody who voted for him meant it as a compliment. They never laughed at his jokes. He was simply the obvious choice.

Gary often daydreamed about being on a late-night talk show, sitting next to beautiful starlets and other celebrities, cracking jokes. Naturally, all the starlets would fall in love with him because he was so funny.

Sometimes Miss Langley would be up on stage with him. . . .

"You were his seventh-grade teacher, weren't you?" asks David Letterman.

"That's right," says Miss Langley. "But even then I knew he'd grow up to be a famous comedian. Of course, as a teacher, I never would let myself laugh at his jokes. I bit the insides of my cheeks raw to keep from laughing. He was so funny. I only wished I was fifteen years younger."

Miss Langley happened to be one of the most beautiful teachers ever to teach seventh-grade math. At night when Gary dreamed about her, he called her Miss Longlegs.

He dreamed about her surprisingly often—at least once a week.

"Hey, Goon!" said Matt Hughes. "Has anybody ever told you you're an idiot?"

"Yes, thank you," said Gary. "Paul mentioned it this morning. Ha. Ha."

2.

Gary wrote a story called "The Boy Who Ate Fire" for English class.

Mrs. Carlisle was his English teacher. Someone in the class had asked how many pages the story had to be. "Whatever's appropriate," Mrs. Carlisle had answered.

That was her big mistake.

THE BOY WHO ATE FIRE
by
Gary W. Boone

Once upon a time there was a boy who ate fire. He died.

Mrs. Carlisle refused to accept the story. "It's not a story," she said. "It's only one sentence."

"Two," corrected Gary.

She told him he had to rewrite the story, and that it had to be at least five pages. She said it was a good title, but it doesn't tell what happens.

"But that's what happens when you eat fire," said Gary. "You die."

It was supposed to be a joke.

Mrs. Carlisle didn't laugh.

Someday, Gary thought, his story would be published. It would be a big thick book and cost $19.95. *The Boy Who Ate Fire* by Gary W. Boone. Then you'd open it up and it would just have two sentences, followed by three hundred blank pages. It would be hilarious. Millions of people would buy it and put it on their coffee tables. He'd be rich.

After English, Gary headed to math class. He'd been in junior high for almost a month, but he still found it muddling to have to change classrooms every period. At night he sometimes dreamed he couldn't remember his schedule. He also dreamed they changed his schedule without telling him.

They changed his locker combination in his dreams too. Once, he dreamed that for some odd reason he had taken off his clothes in the hallway and locked them in his locker because he thought it was his gym locker—although that didn't exactly make sense either. He quickly realized his mistake, standing there in the hallway in his underwear—as Miss Longlegs, wearing cowboy boots and holding an umbrella over her head, walked toward him—but he couldn't get his locker open. In fact, he couldn't remember which locker was his.

In real life, however, he had no problem with his locker, or in finding his way from class to class. But having to rush around changing classes all the time, he felt like he was missing something; like there was something happening that everybody in the school knew about—except him. And there was nobody he could ask. And even if there was somebody to ask, he didn't know the question.

"Gary, why didn't you do the homework?" Miss Langley asked him after class.

He was standing by her desk, wondering if she owned a pair of cowboy boots. "I didn't know about it," he said.

"You didn't know about it? How could you not know about it?"

He shrugged. "There are a lot of things I don't know about. In fact, there are probably more things I don't know about than I do know about." He laughed.

Miss Langley stared at him. "It was on the board," she said slowly and distinctly, like she was talking to an idiot.

"Where?"

"Where it always is," said Miss Langley. "In the box in the upper right-hand corner."

Gary looked at the blackboard. There was a section blocked off which contained the day's homework assignment.

"I've put the homework there every day since the first day of school," said Miss Langley. "Don't tell me you didn't know that."

He didn't tell her.

Miss Langley stared at him in disbelief. "Have your eyes ever been checked?" she asked.

"No," said Gary. "They've always been brown."

In one of his more bizarre daydreams Gary imagined himself as some kind of superhero who caught criminals by telling them jokes. The crooks would laugh so hard they'd fall down.

SUPERGOON CATCHES BANK ROBBERS! *the headline proclaims. The newspaper has a picture of the two masked men laughing hysterically on the sidewalk, while Gary is standing over them, telling one joke after another.*

> *Gary "Supergoon" Boone broke up a bank robbery at the First National Bank this afternoon. The two armed robbers were fleeing from the scene, when Goon shouted out a joke, causing the men to fall over in uncontrollable fits of laughter. Goon bravely continued to crack jokes, despite the guns pointed at his heart, until the police arrived. "I knew they wouldn't shoot," Goon said, "because then they would miss the punch line."*
>
> *For the safety of our readers we cannot reprint any of Goon's jokes. They are so funny they are dangerous. Besides, Supergoon might need to use them again to catch other dangerous criminals.*

Gary never cried. He laughed. The more it hurt, the more he laughed.

Like the time he accidentally bumped into Philip Korbin, making him drop his ice cream bar in the dirt.

"Sorry," Gary said, with a silly grin plastered across his face.

"You think it's funny, Goon?" asked Philip.

"No," said Gary, "ha ha."

Philip pushed him.

"I said I was sorry. Ha. Ha."

Philip pushed him again, and he fell down. He smiled at the crowd that had gathered around.

"Pick it up!" said Philip.

Gary picked up the ice cream bar. The vanilla ice cream was covered with dirt on all sides. "Looks good, ha ha."

"Eat it."

Gary laughed.

"What a goon!" someone said.

"Eat it," said Philip.

Gary licked the dirty ice cream. "Yum chocolate chips," he said. "Ha. Ha."

"All of it," said Philip.

Gary brought it back to his mouth.

Philip grabbed Gary's hair with one hand, and his elbow with the other. He shoved the ice cream bar deep into Gary's mouth. The stick hit against the back of his throat.

Gary continued to laugh as ice cream dripped down his face.

3.

Gary had a girlfriend.

He never told Angeline (that's her name) she was his girlfriend. He never kissed her, except one time on the cheek when she was asleep. Angeline was only ten years old.

But she laughed at his jokes. She didn't just laugh. She howled. Sometimes she rolled around on the floor in hysterics.

"You're the funniest person in the world," she once told him.

"You can't know that," Gary said modestly. "There might be somebody in New Zealand who's funnier."

"No, there isn't," said Angeline. "You're the funniest. I know."

When Angeline spoke like that, Gary believed her. Angeline knew things. Everyone called her a genius—except Gary, because he knew she didn't like to be called that.

He first met Angeline when he was in the fifth grade. She was only eight years old then, but she was put in the sixth grade. She was the smartest person in his elementary school. She was smarter than the teachers.

So if Angeline Persopolis (that's her last name) said he was the funniest person in the world, that meant he was the funniest person in the world. It didn't matter if nobody else laughed at his jokes.

Now Angeline was going to the Manusec School in Nebraska, where she studied astrophysics and nuclear chemistry, then played kickball at recess.

But sometimes, when Gary told his jokes at school, he could hear Angeline laugh a thousand miles away.

He had gone with her to the airport. He remembered standing in the gate area along with Gus, Mr. Bone, and Angeline's father, Abel Persopolis. Everyone was sad. Gary was afraid that Angeline's father was going to cry.

Gary told a joke. "Did you hear about the man who fell out of an airplane—and lived?"

"Did he have a parachute?" asked Angeline.

"Nope." said Gary.

"Did he land in a haystack or something?" asked Angeline.

"Nope," said Gary. "The airplane was on the ground!"

Angeline laughed.

"No, really," Gary said. "There was a guy who fell out of an airplane thirty thousand feet up in the air, without a parachute, and the fall didn't hurt him at all."

"Really?" asked Angeline.

"Really," said Gary. "He was fine the whole time he was falling. But when he stopped falling, boy, that hurt!"

Angeline cracked up.

Angeline's father pointed out to Gary that it wasn't an appropriate time and place to tell jokes about people falling out of airplanes.

"Yes, it is," said Gary. "That's how you keep accidents from happening. You know how to make sure the plane doesn't crash?"

"How?" asked Angeline.

"I don't want to hear this," said Angeline's father.

"It's not a joke," said Gary. "You just think about it crashing. You try to imagine it crashing. You daydream about it crashing. Because," Gary concluded, "daydreams never come true."

⌣

As a child traveling alone, Angeline was the first to board the airplane. She started crying as soon as she went through the gateway. She heard her father calling " 'Bye, Angelini," but she couldn't bear to turn around and look at him.

It would be her first time away from her father. Her mother had died when she was only three.

A stewardess took her hand and led her to her seat.

She didn't want to go to the Manusec School. She wished people didn't think she was so smart.

"My name is Paula," said the stewardess as Angeline sat down. "If there's anything you want, just let me know."

Angeline shook her head, then wiped her face with the back of her hand. She stared out the window. There was nothing she wanted. Except . . . "Paula!" she called.

The stewardess came back to her.

"Do you know any good jokes?" asked Angeline.

4.

Floyd Hicks Junior High School was named after Floyd Hicks, a very wealthy and boring man who was born November 16, 1903, and died January 14, 1969. He donated the property on which the school was built. He also wrote a book about himself. There were ten copies in the school library, and no one, not even the librarian, had gotten past the second chapter.

But it was Floyd Hicks Junior High School, so every November 16 they celebrated Floyd Hicks Day in honor of the great man. This year there would be a talent show, which was ironic because Floyd Hicks had absolutely no talent.

The Spirit Club made posters, and Gary spotted one when he came to school.

CAN YOU SING? DANCE?
OR PLAY THE TUBA?
FLOYD HICKS WANTS YOU!
—IN THE TALENT SHOW

He went straight to the office.

The office was crowded with kids and adults all waiting to speak to Mrs. Walls, the school secretary, who was constantly being interrupted by the telephone. Gary waited nervously. "This is my big break," he muttered.

"What?" said the woman beside him, who was holding a box.

Gary looked at her. "Huh?" he said.

The bell rang.

"Oh, great," he said. "Now I'm late for class."

"Are you talking to me?" asked the woman with the box.

"Huh?" said Gary.

He imagined himself up on stage in the auditorium, jokes rolling off his tongue, and the audience rolling in the aisles. Suddenly he'd become popular. Kids who had never talked to him before started hanging around, waiting for more of his jokes.

"Gary, you're too much!" says Brenda Thompson, one of the more popular girls in the seventh grade.
"Just call me Goon," he replies.

"Yes, Gary?" said Mrs. Walls.

"Just call me Goon," he said.

Mrs. Walls stared at him.

He laughed, then said, "Uh, I want to sign up."

"What?"

The woman next to him set her box down on the counter.

"For the talent show," said Gary. "I want to be in the talent show."

"So?"

"So, how do I sign up for it?"

"I don't know."

"Can you ask somebody?"

Mrs. Walls sighed, then headed to the back of the office. She returned a moment later.

Nobody in the office seemed to know—or care, for that matter. All anyone seemed interested in was why Gary wasn't in class where he belonged.

"All I want to do is sign up for the talent show," he said aloud as he headed to class. Around him, posters urged him to be in the show and show off his talents. First prize would be a one-hundred-dollar savings bond. Second prize would be a twenty-five-dollar gift certificate at Zulu's Records and Tapes. And third prize would be two free sundaes at Maurecia's Ice Cream Parlor.

But none of the posters said where or how to sign up for it.

> **DON'T BE COOL!**
> **MAKE A FOOL**
> **OUT OF YOURSELF**
> **IN THE TALENT SHOW!**

"I know I can do that," he said.

He learned the talent show would be on November 16. He couldn't remember today's date, but he knew the month was October. He figured he had about a month to get ready.

"It'll probably take me that long just to sign up for the stupid thing," he grumbled.

Mrs. Carlisle glanced at him but didn't say anything when he walked in late. The date was on the board: *Tuesday, October 23.* He figured it out at the desk. At first he didn't know if October had thirty or thirty-one days, but then he remembered Halloween was October 31. The talent show would be on a Friday. He had exactly three weeks and three days.

He spoke to Mrs. Carlisle after class. "Do you know where you're supposed to sign up for the talent show?"

Mrs. Carlisle didn't seem to understand the question. "The show is for students, not teachers," she said.

"I know. *I* want to be in the show. Do you know who I'm supposed to tell? I'm not supposed to just walk up on stage without telling anyone, am I?"

"I wouldn't think so," said Mrs. Carlisle, but she didn't know whom he was supposed to tell.

"So'd you hear?" he asked. "They're not making pencils any longer."

"Pardon?"

"They're long enough already!"

Gary sat at his desk in math, looking at Miss Langley but not really listening. It was beginning to feel like a bad dream—one where he just wanted to do something simple, like open his locker, but for some reason could never get it done.

He decided he'd wait until fifth period, gym, and talk to Joe Reed. Joe would know.

"Gary," said Miss Langley as Gary was leaving math class. "The homework assignment is on the board."

He glanced at the board. He knew it was there. He'd already written it down. She didn't have to keep telling him every single day.

"What does she think I am—*stupid?*"

Outside at recess, he decided he couldn't wait until fifth period. What if it was too late? What if Joe was absent?

He spotted Ira Feldman sitting on a planter, looking at his baseball cards.

"Hi, Ira," said Gary.

"Goon," Ira muttered, then looked back at his baseball cards. Ira owned more than a thousand baseball cards, but for some reason had chosen to bring a certain eight of them to school.

"So'd you hear?" asked Gary. "After this year, they're not making bats any longer."

"What? That's crazy. Aluminum bats are no good. Even if you're jammed, you can still get a solid hit. That's—"

Gary had no idea what Ira was talking about. He hadn't said anything about aluminum or wooden bats. "They're long enough already!"

"Huh?"

"They're not making bats any longer. They're long enough already."

Ira proceeded to explain to Gary how different players liked different-sized bats. Rod Carew, for example, used a very short bat, whereas Willie Stargell used a big bat.

Gary nodded along. He didn't know who any of these people were. "So," he said, "do you know anything about the talent show?"

"No, not really."

"Do you know where you're supposed to sign up for it?"

Ira shrugged.

"It's not too late, is it?"

Ira didn't know that, either.

Gary wished he could talk to Angeline. She'd know about the talent show. It didn't matter that she was a thousand miles away in another school. Somehow, she'd know.

Paul Wattenburg, Ryan Utt, and Matt Hughes were sitting on the grass.

"If April showers bring May flowers, what do May flowers bring?" asked Gary.

"Your butt," said Ryan.

"What do you want, Goon?" asked Paul.

"Have you seen Joe Reed?" he asked.

"Yeah, I've *seen* him," said Matt. "I saw him yesterday."

Paul and Ryan laughed.

"So, I was wondering," said Gary, "do you know where you're supposed to sign up for the talent show?"

"Yeah, on your butt," said Ryan.

(Evidently, *butt* was Ryan Utt's favorite word. Probably because it rhymed with his last name.)

"What do you want, Goon?" Paul asked again.

He had just told them. He wanted to sign up for the talent show. "I want to be in the talent show."

"You gonna dance?" asked Matt.

Matt's friends laughed.

"The Dance of the Goon!" said Matt.

They laughed again.

"I'm going to tell jokes," said Gary.

"Well, let's hear one," Paul urged.

Gary thought a second. "What do you call a cow without legs?"

They stared at him.

"Ground beef."

They stared at him.

"You better stick to dancing," said Matt.

"Every morning when I wake up," said Ryan Utt, "the first thing I do is thank the Lord I'm not Gary Boone."

Gary felt a hand on his shoulder. A girl said, "Gary."

He turned around to see Brenda Thompson.

It was probably the first time Brenda Thompson had ever spoken to him. It was certainly the first time she'd ever touched him.

"Did you say you wanted to be in the talent show?" Brenda asked. She seemed genuinely interested.

"If I'm not too late."

"See Miss Langley," said Brenda. "She's the faculty adviser."

"Thanks, Brenda," said Gary.

"Thanks, Brenda," said Paul in a mocking voice, although it was more like he was making fun of Brenda than of Gary.

"Ooooh," said Matt, as if there was something going on between Brenda and Gary.

The boys thought that was hilarious.

Brenda looked scornfully at them. "Get real," she said.

⌣

The talent show had been Brenda Thompson's idea. "It'll be fun," she'd said at the student council meeting.

"I think it sounds stupid," said Philip Korbin, eighth-grade president. "Only an idiot would want to make a fool out of himself in front of the whole school."

"Oh, it'll be fun," Brenda said again.

Most everybody agreed with Philip, but in the end they voted for the talent show because Brenda was popular, and because nobody else had a better idea for celebrating Floyd Hicks's birthday.

But the real reason Brenda had suggested the talent show wasn't because she thought it would be "fun." She just wanted a chance to sing on stage. She imagined herself as the next Madonna.

She never admitted this to anyone. She thought she would say something like, "Well, I guess I *should* be in the talent show, since it was *my* idea. Hmm, what should I do? I don't know. I guess I'll sing."

And it just so happens that on the day of the talent show, a big-time Hollywood producer gets a flat tire while driving through town in his Lamborghini. And while the tire is being fixed he notices a poster for the talent show, so, since he has nothing better to do, he checks it out. When he hears Brenda sing, he immediately rushes backstage and signs her up to do records and movies.

She doesn't even go back to school. She just hops in his red convertible and heads straight for Hollywood with the wind blowing her hair.

"There's only one problem," he says. "It's your name. Brenda Thompson. It's so ordinary."

"I know what you mean," she agrees. "I've always hated it."

"How about if we call you Ruby Goldmine?"

"I love it!"

But all Brenda's daydreams were about to go up in smoke, because the last time she had checked, not one single person had signed up to be in the talent show. She herself wasn't going to sign up for it until some other kids did first.

Imagine how embarrassing it would be, she thought, if she was the only one in the talent show.

‿

When recess ended, Gary was waiting by the door to Miss Langley's room.

"Gary? What are you doing here?"

"I want to be in the talent show," he blurted, almost shouting.

Miss Langley smiled. "Okay," she said quietly.

They went inside. She handed him a clipboard with a piece of paper attached to it. "Sign your name on the list, and next to it put down what you're planning to do in the show."

Gary looked at the blank piece of paper. "There are no other names here."

"You're the first," said Miss Langley.

He smiled as all his worries vanished. He no longer even knew why he had been so worried. After all, there was no reason why he shouldn't be able to sign up for the talent show, just like anybody else.

He held the clipboard high over his head.

"What are you doing?" asked Miss Langley.
"I'm signing *up!*" he said.
He wrote:

Gary W. Boone   *Tell jokes*

(Gary's middle name was Arthur.)

5.

Why did the boy wear a diaper to the party?
Because he didn't want to be a party pooper.

No matter how many times Gary read it, that joke always made him laugh.

He was sitting in his room going through one of his jokebooks. There were twenty-eight books in Gary's bookcase. Twenty-five of them were jokebooks. He also had a dictionary, a book called *Sideways Arithmetic from Wayside School*, which he didn't understand, and a novel about a pirate that Angeline had given him a long time ago and that he'd never read.

"Can I say 'pooper' at school?" he asked aloud.

On the walls of his room were posters of famous comedians: W. C. Fields playing poker, Woody Allen playing the clarinet, Whoopi Goldberg jumping in the air, and one of Robin Williams and Jonathan Winters standing side by side, each trying to look sillier than the other.

He'd once noticed that many of his favorite comedians had a name that began with the letter W. That was why he always signed his name *Gary W. Boone*. If anybody asked, he would say his middle name was Wolfgang, but nobody ever asked.

"Maybe," he considered, "I could get up on stage *wearing* a diaper! 'Hi, my name is Goon. It's wonderful to be here today.' Everybody would already be laughing because of the diaper. 'You're probably wondering why I'm wearing this diaper.' (Pause: One . . . two . . . three.) 'I don't want to be a party pooper!' "

He had once watched a television show where four real comedians talked about how to be a stand-up comic. They all agreed that timing was the most important factor. You should never rush your punch line. As one of the comedians said, "No matter how funny a joke was, it would bomb like a rotten egg if the timing wasn't right." He said that he always paused and counted to three before delivering the punch line.

"Would I really wear a diaper to school?" Gary asked. He shrugged. "Sure, why not?"

Except it wasn't a party, it was a talent show. So party pooper wouldn't make sense. "Or maybe that would just make it even funnier?" He'd have to think about it.

He continued to look through the jokebook.

Why shouldn't you write on an empty stomach?
Because it's better to write on paper.

He wondered how many jokes he'd need. He didn't know how much time he'd have. Normally, a stand-up comic has to fill eight minutes, but it might be different for a school talent show. He didn't know how long it took for him to tell a joke. And how much time should he allow for laughter?

How do you tell a rooster from a hen?
You toss some corn on the ground.
If he eats it, he's a rooster.
If she eats it, she's a hen.

Of course, there was more to it, he realized, than just looking through jokebooks and finding fifteen or twenty funny jokes. The jokes had to be related. One joke had to lead into the next. "Segue" was what the real comedians had called it.

So, after the joke about the hen, he thought he could tell jokes about other animals. "Speaking of animals, did you hear about the frog-jumping contest? My father won." (Pause: One . . . two . . . three.) "He was able to jump over thirty-five frogs."

In his jokebook it was someone named Mr. Jones who jumped over thirty-five frogs, but on television the comics had all agreed it was best to personalize your jokes. You should use members of your family whenever possible.

It was too bad, he thought, that he wasn't old enough to have a mother-in-law. Then he could say his mother-in-law won the frog-jumping contest.

"But seriously, folks, everyone in my family is a good jumper. In fact, I myself can jump higher than my house. I can jump three feet high." (Pause: One . . . two . . . three.) "My house can't jump at all!"

No, instead of saying he could jump three feet high, he realized, it would be better if he just jumped up, right there on stage. It's better if a stand-up comedian is able to move around and do things, rather than just stand up.

What do you do when your nose goes on strike?

Gary's heart jumped as he heard someone enter his room. He slowly closed his jokebook.

"What are you doing?" asked his mother.

He turned around and smiled at her. His parents had a rule. He wasn't allowed to look at his jokebooks until he finished all his homework.

"I don't suppose that's schoolwork," his mother said.

"Sort of," said Gary. "It *is* for school."

People always told Gary he looked exactly like his mother, which bothered him a little bit, not because his mother wasn't nice-looking, but because he didn't want to look like a forty-four-year-old woman. They had the same round face and wide mouth. Their noses were just a bit flat, and they both had small darting eyes.

He told her about the talent show.

"I think that's wonderful," his mother said in a way that didn't sound like she thought it was wonderful.

"First prize is a hundred dollars!" said Gary.

His mother wasn't impressed. "I hope you win," she said. "But your homework comes first. Otherwise I'm going to take all those stupid jokebooks and throw them in the trash. I'm not kidding."

"But this is really important," said Gary. "It's just as important as any of my other schoolwork. In fact, it's more important. *It is!* When I grow up, I'm going to be a stand-up comic. I won't need to know history or math for that."

"That's fine," said his mother. "But right now, I don't want you looking at a jokebook until you finish your homework."

"You know, you're really going to feel silly one day when I'm a famous comedian."

His mother smiled. "I hope you're right," she said. This time she sounded like she really did hope he was right, like maybe it was his only hope.

"So, Mom," he said. "What do you do when your nose goes on strike?"

His mother had already started out the door. "Picket," she answered without turning around.

She'd heard it before. She'd heard them all before.

6.

Joe Reed put his hands on Gary's shoulders and looked him straight in the eye. "Are you going to play seriously," he asked, "or are you going to clown around?"

"I'll play," Gary promised.

"All right!" said Joe as he clapped his hands together.

Gary clapped his hands together too.

Gary liked Joe. He was popular, and a great athlete, but he still treated everyone fairly, even Goon.

Joe was the captain of Gary's flag football team in gym class. For flag football, every player on the team wore a special belt over his gym shorts, with "flags" attached by Velcro. The flags were long plastic strips. Instead of tackling someone, you were supposed to pull one of his flags.

The team huddled around Joe.

Gary had just pretended to pledge allegiance to Joe's flag, which was why Joe asked him if he was going to play or clown around.

Joe looked at Gary. "Can you catch?"

Gary nodded confidently.

"Good," said Joe. "They're not even guarding you. I'll fake a hand-off to Brian, then—"

"I can catch colds," said Gary.

Joe stopped and stared at him. "Can you catch a football?"

Gary tried to think of a funny answer. "With my feet?" he asked.

Joe looked away.

"With your hands, Goon!" said Brian.

"Then why is it called a football?" asked Gary. "Why isn't it called a handball?"

Joe called the play. "All right, Brian, I'll fake it to you, then you flair out to the left flat. Doug and Zack will crisscross over the middle."

"What about me?" asked Gary.

"Hike the ball," said Joe. "On two."

"Yessir!" said Gary. He saluted his captain.

Gary bent down over the ball. On the count of two, he hiked the ball between his legs to Joe. Joe threw it to Zack, who caught it and ran in for a touchdown.

"All right!" Joe cheered. He patted Gary on the back. "Nice hike, Goon. That was good."

"Thanks," said Gary. "Hey, you know why they call it a pigskin?"

Joe was heading down the field.

"Joe, you know why they call it a pigskin?" Gary called after him.

He watched Joe and Zack give each other high and low fives. He wished he'd get a chance to go out for a pass sometime, instead of always having to hike the ball.

7.

Gary rode the elevator up to the fourth floor. The elevator was old and made bumping and creaking noises, like it was ready to break down at any moment. Gary thought it would be fun to be stuck in an elevator and have to be rescued, but despite all its bumping and creaking the elevator never broke down, at least not when he was in it.

He knocked on the door to Angeline's apartment.

Her father opened the door. "Hey, Gary, what's cookin'?" asked Abel Persopolis.

"Mashed potatoes and gravy," Gary replied. He stepped inside. "Where's Angeline?"

Abel looked puzzled. "At her school," he said.

Gary's heart dropped. "But she called me this morning. She said she was home."

"That's impossible," said Abel. "You sure you weren't dreaming?"

He wasn't sure of anything. He shrugged.

"Boo!" shouted Angeline as she jumped up from behind the sofa.

Gary jumped, then laughed.

Angeline laughed too. She was ten years old, but she looked even younger. She only weighed sixty-four pounds.

Gary looked back at her father.

"Gotcha!" Abel said.

Gary smiled. Angeline's father was normally very stiff and serious. It was nice to see him able to clown around.

"So, you know any new jokes?" asked Angeline.

"Does Mother Goose know any nursery rhymes?" said Abel.

Gary smiled. "Okay," he said. "Why did Mrs. Snitzberry stand in front of the mirror with her eyes closed?"

Angeline and her father looked at each other. "I don't know—why?" said Angeline, her face glowing with expectation.

"She wanted to see what she looked like when she was asleep."

Angeline cracked up. She thought it was the funniest joke she ever heard.

Abel smiled, then walked into the kitchen, leaving the kids alone.

Gary and Angeline sat on the sofa. It was also where Angeline slept when she was home. The sofa folded out into a bed.

"I get to come home every weekend!" Angeline announced.

"Wow, that's great!"

"We can start playing croquet again," said Angeline.

"I've got lots of hats," said Gary.

She beamed at him.

"So how's school?" he asked. Then whispered, "You doing anything top-secret?"

"No."

Gary rubbed his chin as he stared at her. "Well, of course you have to say that."

"We don't do anything top-secret," Angeline repeated.

Gary nodded knowingly. "Your secret's safe with me," he said.

"We do mostly boring stuff," said Angeline. "Some of the junk is interesting, but it's like the teachers are trying to fill up our heads with facts. I need to empty my head, not fill it."

Gary nodded. When he was with Angeline, he always felt like he understood what she was talking about, but then when he got home and thought about it, he realized he had no clue.

"My head's empty," he said. "It doesn't help me." He knocked his fist against his head, as if to prove it was hollow.

Angeline laughed.

"There's going to be a talent show at my school," he said.

"Oh, that's perfect!" said Angeline. "You can tell jokes!"

He slapped himself in the forehead. "Now why didn't I think of that?"

"When is it?" she asked.

"November sixteenth."

"Oh, Floyd Hicks's birthday," muttered Angeline. She did some quick calculations in her head, then angrily slammed her fist into the side of the couch. "Bird feathers!" she exclaimed. "Why can't it be on a Saturday? Bird feathers!"

"It's a Friday night," said Gary. "Maybe you can get home in time."

Angeline shook her head. "No, I don't think

so. The airport limo doesn't leave until . . .
Maybe."

"First prize is a hundred dollars," Gary said.

"Oh. Well, that's not important," said
Angeline.

He wondered why she said that. Didn't she
think a hundred dollars was a lot of money?
Or did she just think he had no chance of
winning?

"You should just tell Mrs. Snitzberry jokes
for the talent show," Angeline suggested.
"They're the funniest."

"I don't know," said Gary. "Nobody would
know who she is."

"So, we don't know who she is either," said
Angeline.

That was true. "But we know we don't know
who she is," Gary pointed out.

He had once told Angeline a Polish joke.
As far as he could remember, it was the only
time she didn't laugh. She said she didn't
like ethnic jokes. She thought they were
cruel.

"It was just a joke," Gary had tried to explain, but deep down he realized she was right.

So after that he never told jokes that made
fun of Polish people, or Blacks, or Jews, or

Italians, or any other ethnic group. Instead, he made fun of only one person—Mrs. Snitzberry, whoever she was. The name had just popped into his head.

"Why'd Mrs. Snitzberry always wear two pairs of pants when she went golfing?" asked Gary.

"Why?" Angeline asked eagerly.

"In case she got a hole in one."

Angeline cracked up. "Too bad you're not in my school," she said. "Nobody there tells jokes."

"Right," said Gary. "All I need is an I.Q. of about three thousand."

Angeline blushed and looked away.

"Do you like anybody there?" he asked.

"There's this one girl," said Angeline. "Lola Baines. I like her. She collects worms. She's doing this neat project. She teaches worms to go through a maze. Then she grinds them up and feeds them to other worms. Well, the worms don't really eat the other worms. They ingest them."

Gary nodded like he understood.

"Then the new worms," Angeline continued, "the ones that eat the old worms—they can go through the maze on their first try."

"Really?" asked Gary. "That's amazing. That means— What does that mean?"

"I don't know."

"I wonder," said Gary. "I mean, I wouldn't really do it, so don't worry or anything, but if let's say I chopped you up, and then I ate you, would I be smart?"

"You'd get a stomachache," Angeline said. Then she laughed.

"How can you build a maze for worms?" asked Gary. "I mean, can't they just crawl over walls and stuff?"

"Sandpaper," said Angeline. "They don't like to crawl on sandpaper."

"Oh. That's neat."

Angeline smiled mischievously. "You know what I told Lola?" she whispered. She looked around to see if her dad was listening. "I told her you were my boyfriend."

Gary blushed.

"Is that okay?" Angeline asked.

Gary nodded very quickly.

Angeline smiled at him.

"So," said Gary. "Did you hear about the three prisoners who were going to be executed by a firing squad? They put the first person up against the wall and were about to shoot him, when suddenly he yelled, 'EARTHQUAKE!' While everybody ran for shelter the prisoner got away.

"Well, they finally realized there was no earthquake, so the second prisoner was brought out and put up against the wall. They were about to shoot him, when he yelled, 'TOR-NADO!' Again everyone ran for shelter and the prisoner escaped.

"The third prisoner was Mrs. Snitzberry. They put her up against the wall. 'Ready . . . Aim . . .' And Mrs. Snitzberry yelled, 'FIRE!' "

Angeline laughed so hard she fell off the couch.

Later in the afternoon, Gary went to a movie with Angeline, her father, and Mr. Bone.

Mr. Bone's real name was Melissa Turbone. She had been Gary's fifth-grade teacher. The other kids in the class all called her Miss Turbone. Gary, and later Angeline, called her Mr. Bone. She never knew it because "Mr. Bone" sounded just like "Miss Turbone."

Melissa and Angeline's father had been dating for the last two years. Gary and Angeline hoped they'd get married. It was Melissa who had arranged for Angeline to go to the Manusec School.

"What's cookin', Mr. Bone?" said Gary when Melissa got into the car.

"Mashed potatoes and gravy," she replied.

The movie was about a boy and a dog who ran away from home. Angeline cried during most of the movie.

Gary wished he could cheer her up. "We're on a double date," he whispered into her ear. She stopped crying for a moment and laughed, then continued sobbing at the movie. He almost put his arm around her, but chickened out.

At the end of the movie the boy and the dog came home, the boy's parents hugged them, and everyone was happy. Gary thought that would cheer Angeline up, but instead it made her cry even harder.

"That was the best movie I ever saw," she said when they left the theater.

They all went out to dinner.

Gary had a great time. It wasn't like it was two adults and two kids. They were just four friends out on the town. "So how's the garbage business, Abel?" he asked.

Angeline's father drove a garbage truck. "Not

too bad, Gary," he replied. "We just got a C.D. player for the truck. Except it's hard to hear over the noise. Plus, we have to stop about every thirty seconds, so it's kind of hard to get into a song."

"What kind of music do you listen to?" asked Gary.

"I don't really care," said Abel. "Gus likes country music. And opera. What do you like?"

Gary shrugged.

"People need to recycle more," said Mr. Bone. "We waste so much. At the rate it's going, the garbage dump will be filled up in less than five years. There will be no place to dump."

Gary nodded. He remembered back in the fifth grade Mr. Bone was always talking about recycling, and saving the rain forests, and whales and stuff.

The waitress came by and took their order. Nobody ordered mashed potatoes and gravy.

"Actually, Gary, you want to know what I like best about my job?" asked Abel.

"What?"

"The little kids. I don't know what it is, but little kids love to wave at garbage trucks."

"Do you wave back?" asked Mr. Bone.

"You bet."

"Tell them about the talent show," urged Angeline.

"Our school's going to have a talent show."

"Gary's going to tell jokes!" said Angeline.

He shrugged modestly. "I just hope somebody laughs."

"The important thing is that you do your best," said Gary's former fifth-grade teacher.

"I will," he said. "I've already gone through half my jokebooks. I'm searching for the perfect jokes."

"I thought you were making up your own jokes," said Angeline.

"Anyone can pick jokes out of a jokebook," said Melissa.

"Besides, your jokes would be a lot funnier than any jokes in a jokebook," Angeline said.

Gary thought about it. "Okay, I will!" he said firmly.

"If you're going to do it, do it right," said Melissa. "I know you, Gary. You start things and then don't finish them. You need to give one hundred percent."

"Oh, I will," he assured her. "This is the most important thing I've ever done in my whole life."

"Darn, I wish I could be there for it," said Angeline. "Bird feathers!"

⌣

Brenda Thompson (a.k.a. Ruby Goldmine) was very upset. So far only one person had signed up to be in the stupid talent show: Gary W. Boone.

She said a certain unmentionable word. (She definitely did not say "bird feathers.")

Whatever happened to school spirit? she wondered. Well, if more people didn't sign up, they'd just have to cancel the talent show, that was all there was to it.

(She said that word which was not "bird feathers" again.)

"Julie, why don't you be in the talent show?" she asked.

"Why should I?" asked Julie Rose.

"You could win a hundred dollars."

"Doing what?"

"It doesn't matter. There are no judges. The audience votes on who wins."

They both understood the significance of such a system. It didn't matter whether Julie was talented or not. The voting, like everything else at junior high, would be a popularity contest.

And Julie Rose was possibly the most popular girl in school, though she was going steady with a boy in high school.

"I don't know," said Julie. She blew a strand of hair off her face.

Brenda also tried convincing some of the boys to be in the talent show.

"You're a very talented person, Joe."

Joe Reed shrugged.

"Who all's signed up for it?" asked Paul.

"Uh, well, there's Gary Boone . . ." said Brenda, reading from the paper as if she had a whole list of names. "He's going to tell jokes."

"Goon!" said Matt. "I can tell funnier jokes than Goon."

"Yeah, but you can't tell your jokes in school," said Ryan.

The boys laughed.

Brenda licked her lips.

"You know what we should do?" said Paul. "When Goon is up on stage, telling his stupid jokes, somebody should throw a pie in his face."

"Let's sneak up behind him and pull his pants down," said Ryan Utt.

"Oh, c'mon," said Joe. "You can't do that."

"Why not?" asked Matt.

"It's not right," said Joe. "Think about it. The stupid talent show is probably the biggest thing in his life. Goon doesn't have any friends. All he does is tell jokes. Let him tell his jokes."

"Aw, you're breaking my heart," said Matt.

"Goon's a clown," said Paul. "He'll love it. "We can throw a pie in his face and spray him with a seltzer bottle. I bet he'll laugh right along with everyone else."

"I don't think so," Joe said.

"I say we pants him," said Ryan.

"Well, you're not going to get to do anything to him," said Brenda, "because there's not going to be a talent show if more people don't sign up for it."

"I'm in," said Matt.

"All right, me too," said Joe. "But I say we leave Goon alone. His parents will probably be there and everything."

"Goon has parents?" asked Matt. He screamed in terror.

8.

Gary lay on the floor and looked up at the faces of W. C. Fields, Woody Allen, Jonathan Winters, Robin Williams, and Whoopi Goldberg, almost as if he was waiting for one of them to tell him a joke. They didn't say a word.

He closed his eyes. "Concentrate!" he said. "Jokes. Funny jokes! Jokes nobody ever heard before."

Nothing came to him.

He'd never tried to make up jokes before. They always just popped into his head when he was in the middle of talking.

He sat up. "Okay, then I'll just start talking." He looked around. "What should I talk about?

"I need to stand up to think," he said as he rose to his feet. "I can't make up jokes sitting down. After all, I'm a stand-up comic!"

He clapped his hands. "That's one!" he said. "Now I'm cookin'." He smiled at W. C. Fields. "Now I'm cookin'. What'd the explorer say after he was captured by cannibals and thrown into a pot of boiling water? 'Now I'm cookin'.'"

He turned to Whoopi Goldberg. "All right, that wasn't funny, I admit it, but I'm just getting warmed up. . . . Of course, that's what the explorer said too!"

He walked in circles around his room as he continued to talk to himself.

"Last night we had fish for dinner." (Pause: One . . . two . . . three.) "We fed them worms."

He clapped his hands together. "My mother made spaghetti for the rest of us. You know the difference between a plate of spaghetti and a plate of worms? Well, you better learn if you're ever invited to our house for dinner!

"I had bad breath last night. I guess I shouldn't have put so much garlic on my worms."

He continued to move around the room. He didn't just walk the floor. He stepped up onto his bed, and then over to his chair, and up on top of his desk. He opened his closet door, then stood behind it so that he was squished between the door and the wall. He closed the door and walked out into the middle of his room again.

He didn't seem to be aware that he was doing any of this. His mind was focused on one thing only—making up jokes. His body just moved around on its own, as if separated from his brain.

"I had bad breath once. When I came to school, everybody held their noses. Of course, everyone always does that anyway.

"My breath was so bad, when I said the Pledge of Allegiance, I was arrested for mutilating the flag.

"I don't know why my breath was so bad. Maybe I shouldn't have eaten a dead skunk for breakfast.

"You want to know why I ate a dead skunk for breakfast?

"We were out of pancakes.

"You want to know why I ate a dead skunk for breakfast?

"I couldn't wait till lunch.

"You want to know why I ate a dead skunk for breakfast?

"Because they make too much noise when they're alive.

"Did I tell you I had a girlfriend? Sometimes I'm afraid she thinks I'm ugly. She closes her eyes when she kisses me. I know, lots of people close their eyes when they kiss. It's supposed to be romantic. But she also holds her nose."

Gary stopped. Would he really be able to talk about kissing a girl, up on stage, in front of hundreds of people? In front of his parents?

"Yes!" he asserted. Like Mr. Bone said, if he was going to do it, then he was going to do it right. One hundred percent.

"You know how to tell a girl worm from a boy worm? By kissing them."

He laughed. He thought that was his funniest joke yet, but then when he stopped and thought about it, he realized it didn't make any sense.

That was all right. He had almost three weeks. His plan was to make up jokes every day this week and the next. Then the third week, he'd pick out his best jokes and put them together so that one segued into another; then he'd practice over and over again in order to get his timing just right.

He continued moving around his room for over an hour, talking to himself, brainstorming, or, as he called it, "joke storming." Then he stopped.

It was almost as if an alarm clock rang in his head, telling him it was time to quit. *You're not funny anymore*, it buzzed.

That was fine. Maybe he would be funnier tomorrow. Or the next day? Or next week?

He got out a pad of paper and wrote down what he thought were some of his better jokes.

"Don't bother your father," said Gary's mother. "He's had a very difficult day."

"I'm just going to tell him some of my new jokes," said Gary.

"I think he'd rather just be left alone."

"He'll laugh," said Gary.

Gary's father, still in his suit and tie, was lying on his back on top of his bed and staring at the television. He had managed to take one of his shoes off, but the other was still on his foot, dangling over the side of the bed so as not to get on the bedspread.

"Do you want to hear some of the jokes I made up for the talent show?" asked Gary.

"No."

"I made them up myself. Don't you want to hear them?"

"Gary, I've had a hard day," said his father. "I just want to relax."

He was watching a situation comedy, but he wasn't laughing. He just lay there, staring blankly at the TV screen, while the studio audience cracked up.

Gary sat at the foot of the bed and watched awhile. Somebody got paid a lot of money, he realized, to write the stupid show. He was only a seventh-grader, but he figured he could write a show that was a lot funnier than the one his father was watching.

His mother stood in the doorway motioning for him to leave. He turned back to his father. "C'mon, don't you want to hear the jokes I made up? They're really funny!"

His father let out a heavy sigh.

"Leave your father alone," said his mother.

"Did you hear about the bald eagle who wore a wig?" Gary asked him.

"No!" snapped his father. "Don't tell me. I don't want to hear any of your jokes right now, okay?"

"Too late, I already said it," said Gary. "That was the whole joke."

"I don't want to hear it," his father repeated. "Do you understand?"

"But I already told it to you."

"Do you understand?"

"I was only—"

"Your father is very sensitive about his bald spot," said Gary's mother.

Gary's father sighed even louder. "I am not," he said. He had a bald spot on the back of his head. "I just would like some peace and quiet so I can watch television. Is that too much to ask? Can I just go fifteen minutes without having to listen to one of your idiotic jokes!"

"All right," said Gary, "I won't tell you the joke, even though I already told it to you."

"Thank you."

"You're welcome," said Gary. "Anytime. Ha. Ha."

Gary sat in his room

He wished his parents could be more like Abel and Melissa, who appreciated a good joke when they heard one. At least they'd be willing to listen, after he worked two hours making up jokes for the talent show—the most important day of his life.

If Abel and Melissa were his parents, he realized, then Angeline would be his sister. She was probably more like a sister than a girlfriend anyway.

He'd always wished he had a brother or a sister. Actually, he wanted a sister named Sally. Then he could call her Saloon.

Of course, before Abel and Melissa could be his parents, they'd have to get married. "That's stupid," he said. "They can't be my parents anyway. I already have parents. Unless they got killed in plane crash or something. Ha. Ha."

His father never used to hate jokes. In fact, his father had told him the first joke he ever heard. Gary still had a picture in his mind of himself taking a bath while his father told him a joke. He probably was only three years old. He still remembered the joke.

Why'd the chicken cross the playground?
To get to the other slide.

The odd thing was, Gary figured now as he thought about it, he must have heard that joke before he ever heard the joke about the chicken crossing the road. So it didn't make any sense. But that didn't matter when he was three. He remembered asking his father to tell him that same joke over and over again for months.

There was a knock on the door.

"Come in," he said.

His mother followed his father into the room. Gary didn't look at them.

"Your father and I have been talking," said his mother.

"I understand this talent contest means a lot to you," said his father.

Gary stared out the window at a streetlight.

"I'd like to make a suggestion," his father said.

"How can you make a suggestion?" snapped Gary. "You won't even listen to my jokes."

"I'm sorry if I hurt your feelings," his father said. "I had a tough day, and I just wanted to sit in front of the TV without having to think."

"Well, if you had listened to one of my jokes, it might have cheered you up," said Gary. "Who knows, you might even have laughed. Some people laugh at jokes, you know."

His father smiled. "Okay, tell me the one about the bald eagle who wears a wig."

Gary threw up his hands in frustration. "That's the joke!" he said, trying not to shout. "There isn't any more."

"Oh," said his father. "Well, then how about another one?"

Gary thought a moment. "Why'd the chicken cross the playground?" he asked.

"I don't know," his father said, happy to play along. "Why?"

"You really don't know?"

"No."

Gary shrugged. "I don't know either," he said.

His father laughed awkwardly, unsure if that was a joke or not. "Well, your mother and I have talked it over," he said, "and we'd like to offer a suggestion. We'd like you to try to go the next three weeks without telling any jokes."

Gary looked at them like they were out of their minds. "I'm going to be in the talent show. I have to make up jokes."

"We know that," said his mother. "Just keep them to yourself."

"First prize is a hundred dollars, right?" asked his father. "We'll put a hundred dollars in your savings account if you can make it until the talent show without telling anyone a joke."

Gary laughed. "C'mon," he said. "My jokes

aren't that bad, are they? Ha. Ha. I'm the first stand-up comic who gets paid for *not* telling a joke. Ha. Ha."

"Everything you say is a joke," said his mother. "It stops being funny after a while."

"You should want to keep your jokes to yourself anyway," said his father. "If you tell someone a joke, he'll tell it to someone else, and pretty soon everyone will know it before you ever get a chance to say it at the talent show."

Gary laughed again. "I don't have to worry about that," he said. "Nobody ever repeats any of my jokes. Ha. Ha."

"I do," his father said.

"Really?" asked Gary. "When?"

"Just today," said his father. "I have a client who likes to fish. So I asked him, 'Do you know how to keep fish from smelling?' "

Gary smiled. "Oh, yeah, that's a good one," he said.

Gary's father was a stockbroker. He specialized in something called high-yield mutual funds. He'd tried to explain the stock market to Gary, but it bored Gary senseless.

"So?" Gary's mother asked impatiently. "How do you keep fish from smelling?"

"Cut off their noses," said Gary's father.

Gary's mother cracked up.

"I've told you that joke before!" said Gary. "You didn't laugh when I said it."

She shrugged. "Sorry. It's just . . . I don't know. Coming from your father . . ."

"Did your client laugh?" Gary asked his father.

"Yes, as a matter of fact he did."

"Did he buy lots of stock?"

"No, he didn't buy any."

"But if he laughed—"

"One's got nothing to do with the other," said his father. "That's your problem. You seem to think that the way to be successful, or the way to make people like you, is to tell jokes. But people will like you because of who you are, not for the jokes you tell."

"But that's who I am," Gary insisted. "I tell jokes."

"No, that's not who you are," said his mother. "You tell jokes because you're afraid to let people see who you are. You hide behind a wall of jokes."

"Not a very strong wall," said Gary. "It won't hold up a house. Ha. Ha."

"When you were little," his mother said,

"and we'd have company over, everyone would always ask you to tell jokes because you knew so many."

"Really?" asked Gary. "I don't remember that."

"It was cute because you were four years old. But you're not four years old anymore, Gary."

"You make it sound like I've got some kind of disease or something. Joke-itis. Ha. Ha."

"Just try to go three weeks without telling a joke," said his father. "See what happens."

"And you'll pay me a hundred dollars?"

"That's right."

Gary looked at them. In a way it seemed too good to be true. In another, it made him feel like he'd just eaten a dead skunk. "But how would you find out if I told someone a joke at school or someplace?"

"We trust you," his mother said.

"So, do we have a deal?" asked his father.

"Sure," said Gary. "I'll get the cards."

"What?"

"To deal!" He laughed like a hyena.

9.

Gary crossed the street in front of Floyd Hicks Junior High. He felt like a brand-new person. "The new improved Goon," he said, then laughed. "No, not Goon." He didn't want to be called Goon anymore.

"I don't have to be funny," he said.

It was like he was wearing all new clothes. "No, not new clothes," he said. He still looked the same on the outside. "New underwear! It's like I've been wearing the same pair of under-pants for ten years, and now I've finally gotten a new pair."

He'd just say normal things and make some normal friends. And he'd get a hundred dollars from his parents for not telling a joke, and another hundred when he won the talent show.

He tried to figure out what a normal kid would buy with two hundred dollars. Maybe a Nintendo.

"Hey, Joe," says Gary. "You want to come over after school and play with my Nintendo?"

"Sure, Gary," says Joe Reed.

"Hi, Gary, how're you doin'?" asks Ryan Utt.

"Okay."

"So, Gary," says Matt Hughes. "You got any plans this weekend?"

"Not really."

"Good, why don't you come over to my house? We're going to . . . to . . . to . . ."

Gary's daydream had to end there. He didn't know what normal kids did on weekends.

He and Angeline liked to play croquet.

Ira Feldman was arguing about something with Steve and Michael Higgins. Steve and Michael were twin brothers. All three were holding baseball cards.

Gary joined them. Apparently, Ira was trying to convince one of the Higgins brothers to trade a certain baseball card, while the other Higgins brother was advising against it.

Gary nodded his head several times as he listened to them.

Ira was in the middle of listing all the accomplishments of somebody named Kirby Puckett, when he suddenly turned and asked, "What do you want, Goon?"

Gary shrugged. "Nothing."

Ira returned to his negotiations.

"So, baseball cards, huh?" Gary asked.

"Uh-huh," answered Steve, or maybe Michael. Gary couldn't tell them apart.

"Look," Ira said to Michael (or maybe Steve). "If you don't want to do it, don't do it. Personally, I think I'm doing you a favor, but I'm not going to twist your arm."

"Some favor," said the other Higgins twin.

"What are you talking about?" protested Ira. "The only reason I'm even offering the deal is, I already have four Kirby Pucketts."

Gary laughed.

They all looked at him.

"What's the matter?" asked Ira. "Don't you think it's fair?"

That had nothing to do with it. He just thought Kirby Puckett was a funny name. He thought of a joke about it being foul, not fair, but kept it to himself.

It felt good to not tell a joke, for once.

"What do you think, Goon?" asked Michael (or maybe Steve). "Should I do it?"

Gary shrugged. "Um . . ."

"You're not going to listen to Goon, are you?" asked Steve (or maybe Michael).

"Sure. Whatever he says—I'll do the opposite!"

They all laughed.

"So what do you think, Goon?"

"Um . . ."

He was saved by the bell.

"Well, gotta go," said Gary. "See you later."

He tried hanging out with different groups of people during recess and lunch. He even sat and listened to Janis Carr, Vicki Mathews, and Marsha Posey talk about giving each other permanents. Finally Vicki turned and demanded, "What are you doing here?"

He shrugged. He couldn't think of anything to say, except a joke—"if you really want your permanents to be permanent, you should use concrete instead of hair spray"—but he kept it to himself.

He might as well have told them a joke because when he walked away, he heard them all laughing at him.

"Hey, Joe!" he shouted as he ran out onto the football field.

Joe was talking to Zack, but turned and smiled at Gary. "Hey, what's happ'nin', Goon?"

Gary shrugged and smiled.

Joe continued his conversation with Zack.

"So, how about throwing me a pass today?" said Gary. "No one ever guards me."

"That's because center's not eligible," said Zack. He and Joe laughed.

Joe patted Gary on the back. "You're doing a great job hiking the ball. Keep it up."

"Okay, Joe."

The game started. After each play, Gary was the first one back in the huddle with Joe. "Good pass, Joe," he said. Or, "Nice run." Or, "That would have been a touchdown if he hadn't tipped it."

Joe kept having to move around him so he could talk to the other members of the team.

"So what are you going to call this time, pass

or run?" asked Gary. "How about a triple reverse?"

"Back off," said Joe. "I'll call the plays,"

"Sure, Joe. I understand. I was only trying to help."

Joe put his hands in front of him, almost as if he was going to push Gary out of the way. "If you really want to help, the best thing you can do is just keep out of my face. Okay?"

"Okay, Joe."

10.

It got worse as the week wore on.

"I don't like being called Goon anymore," he told Matt Hughes.

"What, Goon?" asked Matt.

"Just call me Gary. Not Goon."

"Okay, Goon," said Matt.

"I said—"

"I heard you, Goon. I won't call you Goon anymore. Okay, Goon?"

"How about Blubberhead?" asked Paul.

"Lard Butt?" suggested Ryan.

He shrugged and walked away.

He wasn't exactly surprised. He knew he didn't have any friends. It was just that he'd never quite realized before that if he didn't go up to people and tell them a joke, no one ever spoke to him. No one even said "Hi, Goon" to him in the hall.

But he'd made a deal with his parents, and he kept to it. He remembered a poem from a book he'd read when he was a little kid.

> I meant what I said
> And I said what I meant. . . .
> An elephant's faithful
> One hundred per cent!

He told it to himself whenever he was feeling especially depressed, and it always managed to cheer him up a little bit.

After school, alone in his room, he was happy—making up jokes. It seemed the more miserable he was at school, the funnier the jokes. It was like the jokes were building up inside him all day long, bursting to get out. Like Rumpelstiltskin, that wretched soul who spun straw into gold, every evening Gary Boone spun his misery into humor.

He often made up jokes in the shower. He'd stay in there until all the hot water was gone, and then suddenly have to quickly wash himself under the freezing spray.

He never decided beforehand what his jokes would be about. He'd just start talking, and out they'd pop.

Wednesday was October 31, Halloween. He might have guessed he would make up jokes about ghosts or witches, but instead, on Halloween night he made up a Christmas joke. He thought it was his funniest joke yet, but then again, they were all hilarious.

He had no doubt he would win the talent show.

"Either that, or I'll totally flip out and turn into some weirdo or something. Just sit in a corner and pick my nose all day." He laughed. "Or maybe I'll shave my head, get a machine gun, and blow away half the school. Ha. Ha."

As they bury the dead the newsmen try to figure out why a young lad, only twelve years old, would do such a horrible thing.

"He seemed harmless," says a classmate.

"He didn't have a lot of friends. He kept to himself."

"He didn't like baseball cards."

"He liked to tell jokes. I guess we should have laughed."

"I guess we should have laughed," repeats the TV newsman, in a serious and ominous voice.

Even Gary had to stop and wonder about himself for a moment after that one.

"Do you feel like an egg this morning?" his mother asked him Friday morning when he came down for breakfast.

He looked at her curiously. Was she testing him?

Do you feel like an egg this morning?
I don't know. How does an egg feel?
Do you feel like an egg this morning?
Just call me Humpty Dumpty.
Do you feel like an egg this morning?
Yes. You better not drop me. I might crack.

"No thanks," he said. "I'll have cereal."

On his way to school, he suddenly stopped right in the crosswalk in the middle of the street in front of Floyd Hicks Junior High. He looked at the two-story building, the kids in the schoolyard, the buses in the parking lot. Until he stopped telling jokes, he'd never realized just how much he hated school.

A car honked at him.

He didn't move.

Another car sped around him.

Why'd the Goon cross the road? he wondered.

"I don't have a dog, but I've always wanted one. So I got a goldfish. His name's Rover.

"I've taught him to fetch a stick. You know how some people throw sticks in the water for their dogs to chase. I throw a stick out of the water for Rover to chase."

Gary stepped down from on top of his chair.

At first he thought a fish named Rover was a great idea, but now he couldn't think of any more jokes. That was okay. That happened. He just had to go on to something else. Maybe a fish joke would pop into his head later. Maybe when he was sleeping. Sometimes when he woke up in the morning, he'd suddenly think of a new punch line for a joke he had started the night before.

He continued walking around his room. "Did I tell you about my father? He's very handy around the house. Always fixing things. Yesterday he hooked up a new VCR. He also put in a garage door opener. It all works great. Except every time you push the button on the remote control to change the channel—the garage door opens.

"Last week he fixed the toilet and installed

76

a new light switch in the bathroom. Now if you want to flush the toilet, you have to flick the light switch. And if you want to turn on the light, you have to push the lever on the toilet.

"I have a sister named Sally. Everyone calls her Saloon. She's disgusting, although I guess I shouldn't say bad things about her." Gary put his hand over his heart. "She's in the hospital.

"She needs a tongue transplant.

"It's 'cause she never stops talking. She's sixteen years old and this will be her third tongue!

"She was talking on the phone to one of her boyfriends. She was in the middle of telling him how much she loved him, when her tongue flapped out of her mouth and onto the floor.

"I was there, sitting at the kitchen counter having a snack. It was disgusting. Not her tongue. I mean my sister saying, 'I love you, sweetheart,' right there on the kitchen phone while I was trying to eat.

" 'Course, without her tongue it didn't sound like, 'I love you sweetheart.' It sounded more like, 'I uv you, wee-har.'

"Her boyfriend probably didn't even notice.

They're always talking baby talk to each other. I told you she was disgusting.

"Meanwhile, the tongue flapped around on the floor for a while, like a fish out of water, until it finally stopped and lay still.

"My dad came in to get a glass of milk and stepped right on it.

"Have any of you ever stepped on a tongue?

"No? Well, it's like a banana peel, except thicker and more slippery. My dad desperately tried to hold on to the quart of milk as he went flying."

No, not quart of milk. Half gallon. "Gallon of milk." The more milk, the funnier.

"Meanwhile, my sister just went right on talking as she glared angrily at my father, who was lying on the floor in a pool of milk. Finally she held the phone aside and said, 'I'm trying to talk on the phone, if you don't mind!' Except it sounded like, 'I'm rying oo auk ah uh pho, if you o mi!'

"We tried to pick up the tongue, to show it to her, but it kept slipping through our fingers.

"Have any of you ever tried to pick up a tongue after it's been covered in milk?

"No? Well, it's like soap in a bathtub. Just

when you think you have it, it squishes out of your hand and goes shooting across the room.

"My sister finally hung up. As she walked across the kitchen floor I thought she was going to step on it too.

" 'Watch your tongue!' said my father.

"She just gave him a dirty look, then bent down and picked it up. She had no problem picking it up because she has long fingernails.

"Then she slapped me across the face with it. She just kept hitting me, over and over again. She gave me a real tongue-lashing.

"My mother came in and said, 'Hold your tongue, young lady.'

"So now she's in the hospital, waiting for a suitable donor. This time she says she wants a giraffe tongue. She heard those are the best for kissing.

"Her old tongue is on my dad's desk, stapled to his blotter. He keeps it moist and uses it for wetting stamps and envelopes."

11.

Gary knocked on the door to Angeline's apartment. He was wearing a hat.

Gus answered the door.

"Hey, Gus, what's cookin'?" said Gary.

"Mashed potatoes and gravy," said Gus.

Gus was also wearing a hat.

Gus was probably older than Angeline's father, but in a lot of ways he seemed more like a kid than an adult. He was Abel's partner. Sometimes Gus drove the garbage truck while Abel picked up the garbage, but usually it was the other way around because Gus liked to look for what he called buried treasure.

Gus was wearing an Australian safari hat

with a camouflage band. Gary was wearing a black derby.

"Nice hat,"said Gus.

"Thanks," said Gary. "I like yours, too."

"Would you believe it?" asked Gus. "Someone actually threw it in the trash."

"You're lucky!" Gary said. "I paid three bucks for mine!"

Gary had been to Gus's house once. It was full of incredible stuff that other people had thrown away.

Angeline came out of the bathroom wearing a pink cowgirl hat with little gold tassels dangling from the brim. "What's cookin', Gary?" she asked.

"Mashed potatoes and gravy."

Abel had on a black beret.

They all went to the park and played croquet.

It was Gus's croquet set. Just because one of the mallets was broken and a few of the wickets were missing, someone had actually thrown it in the trash. New wickets had since been made out of wire hangers (also thrown away), and if there weren't enough mallets to go around, they simply shared.

The first time they played, Gus had to teach

everyone the rules. He said, "The first rule of croquet is, you have to wear a hat." He had brought hats for everyone.

Now they all had their own hats. Gary stopped at a thrift store at least once a week to check out the hats. He was constantly adding to his collection.

They each had their own peculiar styles of playing croquet too. Gus would just wallop the ball as hard as he could on every shot, no matter how close he was to the wicket—although he hardly ever aimed for a wicket. When you play croquet, you usually aim either for a wicket or for somebody else's ball. Gus almost always tried to hit somebody else.

Angeline would hold her mallet high above one shoulder and then swing down at the ball, like a pendulum, so that when she finished, the mallet would be high above the other shoulder. She alternated, one time hitting the ball from the right side, the next time from the left. The most important thing seemed to be not breaking the rhythm of the pendulum.

"I don't see how you can swing like that," said Gary, "and still always hit the ball so straight."

Angeline shrugged. "You have to be the ball," she explained.

"Huh?" said Gary.

"You're being the mallet," she said. "You have to try to be the ball."

Abel would walk around like a golfer, studying the angles and the slope of the field. He thought about each shot a long time, and then finally took the shot. More times than not, he'd *just* miss the wicket. Sometimes he'd aim for someone else's ball, but never his daughter's.

Gary never held the mallet the same way twice. Sometimes he held it way down on the shaft, other times high up; sometimes with his left hand on top of his right, sometimes reversed. Sometimes he'd swing the mallet through his legs, other times off to the side. He once tried Angeline's method, but missed the ball entirely.

He didn't know how to "be the ball." He had a hard enough time "being the mallet," whatever that was supposed to mean.

"Okay, Gary," said Gus. "I think I got you this time. Why'd Mrs. Snitzberry tiptoe past the medicine cabinet?"

Gary shrugged.

There was stunned silence.

"Hah!" exclaimed Gus, clapping his hands together. "I knew I'd get you one day, Gary Boone!"

He smiled.

Gus was so happy he had finally stumped the great Gary Boone, he forgot to finish his joke.

"Why did Mrs. Snitzberry tiptoe past the medicine cabinet?" Angeline asked impatiently.

"Oh," said Gus, "she didn't want to wake up the sleeping pills."

Angeline laughed.

Of course Gary knew the punch line. He just wasn't allowed to tell jokes. In fact, not only did he know Gus's punch line, he knew an even better one:

Why'd Mrs. Snitzberry tiptoe past the medicine cabinet?
She didn't want to embarrass the "Bare" Aspirin.

"Bird feathers!" exclaimed Angeline as Gus's ball crashed into hers.

Gus placed his ball next to her ball, stepped

on his ball, then slammed his mallet against it, knocking her ball to the far end of the court.

"One of these days you're going to break your foot that way," said Abel.

Gus laughed. He turned to Angeline. "That ought to keep you busy for a while."

She stuck out her tongue at him.

He stuck out his tongue back at her.

For hitting Angeline's ball, Gus got another shot. He aimed for the wicket but missed, and his ball kept rolling until it was almost as far away as Angeline's.

"Bird feathers!" he exclaimed.

"So what's the deal, Gary?" asked Abel. "How come you haven't told us any jokes?"

"Oh, sure he has!" Angeline said. She looked at her father like he was crazy.

"No, I haven't" said Gary.

"Really?" asked Angeline.

He told them about his deal with his parents.

Gus thought it was a "bum deal," but Angeline agreed with Gary's parents. "If you keep all your jokes bottled up inside, then when they come out, they'll be even funnier. Like a balloon. The more air that's forced inside, the louder the pop!"

"That's right!" said Gary. "That's exactly what happens. I don't tell any jokes at school, but then when I get home, they all burst out of me."

"Oh, I wish I could hear them," said Angeline. "But don't tell me."

"I won't," he assured her.

"I'd like to meet your parents," Abel said. "They sound very interesting."

"Huh?" said Gary.

"Do they like to play croquet?" asked Gus. "Why don't you ask them to join us next time."

Gary couldn't imagine his parents spending time with Abel and Gus—especially not Gus. "They don't like to wear hats," he said.

"So you sound really serious about this talent show," said Abel.

"I've been making up jokes all week. My plan is to make up jokes for two weeks and then choose my best ones."

"La crème de la crème," said Gus.

Gary laughed. "Then the last week, I'm going to just work on putting the jokes in some kind of order, and then practice them over and over again. People think that to be a comedian all you need are good jokes, but timing is just as important."

"The important thing is, you're willing to work at it," said Abel. "It doesn't really matter how much talent you have. You have to be willing to work at it. Nothing comes easy."

"I'm working at it, all right," Gary said. "My motto is: Whatever it takes, one hundred percent!"

Gary and Angeline were alone on her sofa. Gus and Abel had gone to get pizza.

"Did you ever wish you could be somebody else?" asked Gary.

"Like who?"

"Joe Reed," said Gary. "Do you know who he is?"

"He was in Mr. Bone's class," said Angeline.

"He's got the perfect life," said Gary. "Everyone likes him. He's smart, a great athlete, but he's not stuck up or anything. He's nice to everybody. Sometimes I wish I was him."

"Maybe you are him," Angeline said. "Maybe he's you."

"Huh?"

"Maybe just this second, when you said you wanted to be Joe Reed, you suddenly traded places. You're now Joe Reed. He's Gary Boone.

But it doesn't matter. I'm still here talking to Gary Boone. He became you. He has your body. Your brain. Your memory. He doesn't remember ever being Joe Reed. He thinks he's always been you. And you think you've always been him. So even though you just traded places, nothing's changed."

"Yeah," said Gary. He saw her point. At least he thought he did. On second thought—he had no clue.

"No matter how many times you trade," she said, "there's always going to be a Gary Boone."

She smiled at him, apparently glad there would always be a Gary Boone. She took off his hat, then placed her pink cowgirl hat on his head. She put Gary's hat on her head.

"So I guess I should just try to be the best Gary Boone I can be," he said. He shrugged. "I may be a goon, but I'll be the best goon there is."

"Whatever it takes, one hundred percent," said Angeline.

12.

Gary woke up feeling funny. Not sick-funny. Funny-funny. Hilarious-funny! Supercalifragilisticexpialidociously-funny!

He felt like he could make up the funniest jokes of his life. The jokes were exploding inside him, ready to burst out, like Angeline's balloon.

But first he had to get through school—six hours of mind-numbing, maggot-infested drivel.

There was a book report due in first period. This was the first time Gary had heard about it.

Fortunately, it was only supposed to be an oral report, so as long as Mrs. Carlisle didn't call on him, he was safe.

Unfortunately, he was the first person called.

"I'm not ready," he said. "I didn't know about it."

"You didn't *know* about it?" Mrs. Carlisle asked incredulously. "Ashley. When did I assign the book report?"

"Three weeks ago," said Ashley.

"Three weeks," Mrs. Carlisle repeated. "Where have you been for the past three weeks, Gary?"

"I don't know."

"I don't know either," said Mrs. Carlisle.

Gary laughed along with several other kids in the class.

"I don't think it's funny," said Mrs. Carlisle. "I think it's sad. I will call on you again, on Friday, and by then I expect you to have a book report ready. And Gary," she added, "not a jokebook this time."

Gary sighed. She didn't have to say that. The first time she assigned a book report, at the beginning of the year, she didn't say it couldn't be a jokebook, so how was he supposed to know? Now he knew. She didn't have to mention it *every single time.*

"What does she think I am—*stupid?*"

And besides, he thought, how am I supposed to know where I was three weeks ago when she assigned the book report? Maybe I was in the bathroom. It's not like she's been talking about it every second for three weeks. It's just like a murder mystery. Where were you at exactly 8:23 on the night of July 13? How's anybody supposed to remember? Only the murderer knows. The innocent people don't remember things like that.

He talked to Miss Langley before class started.

"Yes, Gary?"

"May I see the list?"

"What list?"

"For the talent show."

"I wish you cared as much about math as you do about the talent show."

"I just want to see if anybody else has signed up yet."

"You're not the only one," Miss Langley assured him. She showed Gary the list.

Gary W. Boone	*Tell jokes*
Susan Smith	*Acrobatics*
Joe Reed	*Rap*

Matt Hughes	*Tell jokes*
Brenda Thompson	*Sing*
Julie Rose	*Poetry*
Alex Roth	*Piano*
Leslie Ann Cummings	*Sing*
Connie Lee	*Sing and play guitar*
Fred Furst	*Bird imitations*
Marsha N. Posey	*Roller-skate*

"I don't want to be first," said Gary.

"Pardon?"

"Just because I was the first to sign up, I don't want to have to be the first one up on stage."

"That's not up to me," said Miss Langley.

"Who's it up to?"

"Brenda Thompson, I believe."

Gary nodded and said, "Oh."

"Gary," Miss Langley said gently. "I wouldn't get my hopes too high about the talent show."

He shrugged.

"No offense," Miss Langley continued, "but telling jokes isn't exactly a talent—like singing, or playing the piano, or even *bird calls*. I'm sorry."

"I just hope somebody laughs," said Gary. Then he went to take his seat.

"Gary! Hey, Gary!"

Gary turned. It was Steve (or maybe Michael) Higgins.

"Look what I got!" said Steve (or Michael), waving a baseball card in Gary's face.

"Oh, a baseball card," said Gary.

" 'A baseball card,' he says," said Steve (or Michael). "It's not just a baseball card! Look at it!"

Gary looked at it again. "Bob Bremly," he read aloud. Gary'd never heard of Bob Bremly, but he didn't want to disappoint Steve (or Michael). "Great!" he said, trying to sound excited. "He's a great player, all right."

"No he isn't," said Steve (or Michael). "There is no Bob Bremly. Bob *Brenly* was a catcher for the Giants. But see, they spelled his name wrong. It should be Brenly, not Bremly."

"Oh. Well, maybe you could take it back and they'll give you a new one."

"Are you kidding? Ira already offered me fifty bucks for it, but I wouldn't sell it for less than two hundred. That's how much you'd have to pay at a card show."

"So it's good they spelled his name wrong?" asked Gary.

"It's great! And would you believe it? I got it in just a regular pack of baseball cards!"

Gary smiled politely. He had no idea why Steve (or Michael) was showing this to him.

"So, do you collect baseball cards?" asked Steve (or Michael).

"No," said Gary.

"Oh," said Steve (or Michael). He seemed disappointed. "You should."

Gary shrugged.

"Well, see ya, Gary," said Steve (or Michael).

" 'Bye," said Gary. He continued on to math.

What was that supposed to mean, he wondered, "You *should*"? Collecting baseball cards was something you either wanted to do or didn't want to do. It wasn't something you *should* do. "Why should I?" he asked aloud.

He caught up to Joe on the way to the football field. "So Joe," he said. "I hear you're going to be in the talent show."

Joe laughed. "Big deal," he said.

"Me too," said Gary.

"I know."

"So you're going to do a rap, huh?" said Gary. "Sounds cool."

"Just fooling around, you know how it is," said Joe.

Gary didn't know how it was, but he was glad Joe thought he did. "I'm going to tell jokes. I'm making them all up myself. But I can't tell you any. I'm keeping them all inside so they pop out like a balloon."

Joe looked at him a moment, like he wanted to tell Gary something, but then just smiled. "Sounds cool," he said. He turned away and quickened his pace.

"Thanks," said Gary, staying with him. "Hey, how about letting me do something today, besides just hiking the ball."

"Sure, maybe," said Joe.

"Do you know if Matt is making up his own jokes, or is he just telling jokes he already knows?" asked Gary.

"What?" snapped Joe. He stopped walking and turned on Gary. "I don't know! Why don't you ask him?"

Gary shrugged. "Could you do me a favor? Could you tell Brenda Thompson I don't want to be first? Just because I was the first to sign up for the talent show doesn't mean I want to be on stage first."

"What are you talking about?"

"Brenda Thompson decides the order. You

know—which act goes on first, second . . . Tell her I don't want to be first."

"Why don't—" Joe stopped. He put his hand on Gary's shoulder. "Look, don't take the talent show so seriously, okay? It's for fun. We're all just going to get up on stage and make big fools out of ourselves. It's just for fun."

"Yeah, I know."

"Well, don't be so uptight about it, okay?" Joe said. "Go with the flow. No matter *what happens.*"

"Sure," said Gary. "So will you talk to Brenda Thompson for me?"

"Sure," said Joe.

When Gary got home, he started reading the book about the pirate and the beautiful girl that Angeline had given him a long time ago. He didn't make up any jokes. He had too much work to do. And he no longer felt funny.

13.

Miss Langley assigned four pages of math homework.

Just pour it on, Longlegs! thought Gary. You're the faculty adviser for the talent show, but you don't care if I have time to make up jokes!

He went to see her after class.

"No one else has signed up since yesterday," she said.

He shrugged. That wasn't what he was going to ask her. He started to leave, then stopped. "This isn't the only class I have, you know," he said.

"Pardon?"

"Four pages is a lot of homework. Other teachers assign homework too. I have to read a whole book and do a book report by Friday. How am I supposed to work on my act for the talent show if I have to waste all my time doing *homework?*"

"Maybe if you had started that book report when it was first assigned three weeks ago, you wouldn't have this problem."

He couldn't believe it. How'd she know that? He would have thought that teachers had better things to do than talk about him.

"Goon, over here!" Joe Reed called to him as he stepped out of class.

Joe was standing out by the library. No one else was near.

"I thought of a great idea for a football play," said Joe. "If you're up for it."

"Sure," said Gary.

"No clownin' around?"

"No clownin' around," Gary assured him.

Joe checked to make sure no one else was listening, then told Gary the play. "Now, you're sure you can catch?" he asked.

Gary nodded confidently.

At least he hoped he could catch. It had been a long time since anyone had thrown a football to him. For the first time since he'd seen the poster advertising the talent show, Gary thought about something else. He tried to imagine himself catching the football and running for a touchdown.

He tried not to think about it. It was like he had said at the airport. Daydreams never come true. If you imagine something happening, then it never happens that way.

It was all he thought about, and all he didn't think about, until fifth period.

When the bell rang, he walked confidently toward the locker room. He wasn't a goon. He was part of Joe's team.

"Hi, Goon," said Matt Hughes.

"How's it goin', Goon?" asked Paul Wattenburg.

He shrugged.

Ever since he had told them he didn't want to be called Goon anymore, they said "Hi, Goon" to him whenever they saw him. At least they said "Hi" to him. That was something.

"I'm ready," he told Joe as he joined the huddle.

Joe ignored him. For the first play, Joe called a pass to Zack over the middle.

"What about me?" asked Gary.

"Just hike the ball, Goon."

After each play, Gary looked to Joe, but Joe kept telling him to hike the ball. He seemed to have forgotten all about their special play.

What made it even worse was that nobody else seemed to be playing very well. Zack had dropped two passes. Brian missed one. Joe had been sacked twice. They were losing six to nothing.

Joe looked desperately around the huddle. "Anybody got any ideas?" he asked. "Goon? What about you?"

He felt a knot in his stomach.

"Can you catch?" asked Joe.

"Sure, no problem."

Joe sighed. "Nothin' else seems to work. Play halfback. Take two quick steps to the side, and I'll throw you a short pass, then you follow Zack around the end. Brian, you hike."

It all happened very fast. Brian hiked the ball.

Gary took two steps and turned, but the ball was already there. It bounced off his face.

Joe was furious. "I thought you said you could catch!" he shouted. He shook his head in disgust. "You're supposed to use your hands, not your face!"

His teammates laughed.

"Sorry," said Gary. "It came too fast."

"Oh, gee," said Joe. "Next time I'll under-hand it to you."

They returned to the huddle. "Sorry," Gary said again.

Joe called the next play—a long pass to Brian. "You hike, Goon."

Gary hiked the ball, but way too short. It hit the ground a foot in front of Joe, and the play was dead.

"Can't you even hike the ball?" Joe asked him. "Okay, same thing," he called, without even bothering to go back to the huddle. "Except someone else hike."

"Where do you want me to play?" Gary asked.

"I don't care!" snapped Joe. "You can't catch! You can't even hike the stupid ball! Just get out of my sight, Goon. I don't want to see your face."

Gary walked with his head down almost to

the sidelines—*almost*. When the ball was hiked, he turned and ran upfield.

No one was covering him. No one was near him. This was his play, exactly as Joe had planned it.

He looked over his shoulder as Joe released the ball. It came spiraling through the air.

He knew he'd drop it. He had known it all along. When Joe asked him first thing in the morning if he could catch—he knew then he'd drop it.

But in the back of his mind, he heard Angeline say, "You have to be the ball," and for a nanosecond he understood. The ball came down. His hands went out to meet it, and he gently cradled it against his chest.

Everyone was charging toward him now, but he never broke stride as he continued running across the goal line for a touchdown.

He held the ball in front of his face and stared at it as if he didn't know how it got there. Then he spiked it.

"My man!" shouted Joe as he slapped Gary's hand high in the air.

One by one the players on both teams realized what had happened. It had all been an act—the dropped ball, the bad hike. The Goon had tricked them.

"Why didn't you at least tell your own team?" asked Zack.

"I didn't want anyone to give it away," Joe said.

"Man, that was great!" said Brian. He looked at Gary. "You should be an actor!"

Gary was still out of breath. "It was a great pass," he said. "I'm just glad I didn't drop it."

"Perfect," said Zack. "It wouldn't have worked with anyone else, but everyone already thinks you're a goon. No offense. That's just what everybody thinks. You know that. That's why it worked so well."

"I know," said Gary.

Zack held up his hand and Gary slapped it.

"There's a lot we don't know about old Goon," Joe said. He grabbed the back of Gary's neck and playfully shook it, like a puppy. "I think he's just been sandbagging us all along."

14.

Gary rubbed his hands over his face as he stood in front of his open locker, which was crammed with books. He tried to remember what he needed to bring home.

He was still pretty excited about his touchdown, but he had more important things to think about—jokes. He hadn't made up any jokes yesterday, so he had to make up twice as many today.

He pulled out his math book, then slammed his locker shut before the rest of the books could fall. He still had to finish reading the pirate book too.

Ira Feldman laughed.

Gary turned.

"Michael told me what you said," said Ira.

Gary didn't know what he was talking about.

"Maybe you can take it back and they'll give you a new one," Ira said in a dumb-sounding voice that was supposed to be an imitation of Gary's.

Gary remembered the "Bob Bremly" baseball card that one of the Higgins twins had showed him.

"So Michael says you're going to start collecting baseball cards," said Ira.

Gary shook his head. "No."

"Oh," said Ira. "You should."

There it was again. Why in the world *should* he collect baseball cards? "I collect hats," he said.

Ira looked at him, studying Gary like he might study one of his baseball cards. "Why do you always tell jokes?"

Gary shrugged. He didn't bother to tell Ira that he'd actually stopped telling jokes. "To make people laugh."

"Why?" asked Ira.

He shrugged again. "People like to laugh."

Ira thought about it for a moment. "Yeah, I guess you're right," he said, like it was true for other people though not necessarily for him.

Gary walked away talking to himself. "Why do I like to make people laugh? What kind of question is that? Everyone likes to laugh. It's good to laugh. I should ask Ira why he collects baseball cards, that's what I should do."

"Goon, think fast!"

A football was coming at his face. He held up his math book just in time. The ball hit it and knocked it out of his hands.

Joe and Zack laughed.

Gary laughed too as he picked up the ball.

"Goin' long!" said Zack. Then he took off.

It took a moment for Gary to realize what he was supposed to do, and by then Zack was too far. Gary threw it as hard as he could, but the ball landed way short as Zack ran back to try and catch it.

"You want to go play some football?" asked Joe.

"Me? Sure."

Zack threw the ball back to him. Gary planted his feet and waited to catch it, but Joe jumped in front of him and intercepted.

Joe then immediately lateraled it behind his

back to Gary, but Gary wasn't ready and it bounced off his stomach.

He picked up the ball, then his math book, and ran after Joe and Zack.

"C'mon, you guys. Hustle your butts!" shouted Ryan Utt from the football field.

They had all heard about Gary's trick play in gym class.

"That's great, Goon," said Paul. "I didn't think you had it in you. I didn't know you even knew how to catch."

"Or even which way to run with the ball after you caught it," said Matt.

Everyone laughed, even Gary.

"That's his secret," said Joe. "He's just pretending to be a goon. You're just sandbagging everyone, aren't you?"

Gary smiled. He wished he knew what Joe meant by that.

There was an odd number of players, and after much discussion it was decided, "in order to be fair," that Gary would be the designated center for both teams.

"Just until someone else comes," said Joe. "You understand?"

"Sure," Gary said. "But I can catch, too. I caught that touchdown—"

"Everyone already knows the trick play," said Zack. "It won't work twice."

"Zack and I have been playing together a long time," Joe explained. "I know his moves."

"Besides, what's wrong with playing center?" asked Paul. "You get to handle the ball on every play."

"That's right," agreed Brian. "I sometimes go half a game without even getting to touch the ball."

"It's the most important position on the team," said Matt. "It starts every play."

Gary shrugged. He really didn't mind playing center so much. But if it was such a great position, how come nobody else wanted to do it?

"What do they think I am—*stupid*?"

"You know the most important rule about playing center?" Ryan asked him.

"What?" asked Gary.

"Don't let your butt get in the way of the ball!" said Ryan, then he cracked up.

Gary laughed too. He didn't want Ryan to think he didn't get the joke—even though he didn't.

It was tackle, and everyone played a lot rougher than in gym class. Every time Gary hiked the ball, somebody knocked him back-ward.

"Hey, Goon!" said Matt. "What do you call a snake that's about a foot long and has scaly green skin and two sharp fangs?"

"I don't know."

"I don't know either," said Matt, "but it just crawled down your pants!"

Gary had heard it before, but he laughed anyway. Actually, he'd expected Matt to say, "It's crawling on your neck." He had to admit that "down your pants" was funnier than "on your neck."

But Gary had also thought of two other punch lines.

What do you call a snake that's about a foot long and has scaly green skin and two sharp fangs?
Sir.
What do you call a snake that's about a foot long and has scaly green skin and two sharp fangs?
Cecil.
Why Cecil?
Because that's his name.

I'm sharp today, he thought. I'm so sharp I have to be careful I don't cut myself.

He realized he should have been home making up jokes. Now all he'd really have time to do was go home, eat dinner, do his math homework, and finish reading the pirate book.

Well, what's one day? he thought. One day doesn't matter. Besides, friends are important too.

He hiked the ball; then Paul knocked him backward.

15.

Gary clapped his hands together. He was alone in his room, except for Whoopi Goldberg, Robin Williams, Jonathan Winters, Woody Allen, and W. C. Fields. "All right," he said. "Here we go. The funniest jokes in the world!"

He glanced at the book on his desk. He still hadn't finished reading it, and he had to give his book report in just two days. That's okay, he thought. He had time.

"A duck walked into a doctor's office. The doctor said, 'What seems to be the problem?' The duck said . . .

"The duck said . . .

"What'd the duck say?

"The duck didn't say anything! He had laryngitis!" Gary rubbed his hands together. "That's why he went to the doctor! No, not laryngitis. Quack-ingitis! Yeah, that's funny. Quack-ingitis. No it isn't." He sat on his bed. "Okay, no ducks."

He had expected that he might have a little trouble getting started, since he'd gone two days without making up jokes. No problem. It would take some time to get back in the flow.

Joe and Zack had asked him to play football again after school, but he turned them down.

"You won't have to play center the whole time," Joe had promised.

"I can't," Gary had said. "I got a stupid book report due Friday, and I haven't even read the stupid book yet."

"So, today's only Wednesday," said Zack.

"Sorry," said Gary. "But thanks for asking."

"Whatever," said Joe.

He didn't tell them about having to make up jokes for the talent show. He knew Joe would tell him he was taking it too seriously.

He continued to try to make up jokes. "I went to the doctor today. I said, 'Doctor, you've got to help me. My nose doesn't smell.'

"He told me to take a shower. He said, 'Your nose may not smell, but the rest of you sure stinks!' "

He shook his head. "Well, that joke stinks anyway.

" 'How'd you break your nose?' 'I walked into a door.' 'Didn't you look where you were going?' 'I didn't think it was necessary. The door's usually open. Some *idiot* must have closed it.' "

He thought that was a good idea for a joke, but it just didn't sound funny when he said it. Joe wouldn't think it was funny.

That became the new test. After each joke, Gary tried to decide if Joe would think it was funny.

" 'Doctor, you've got to help me. My nose has turned into a flower. What should I do?' 'Take two aspirin and water it twice a week.' "

No, Joe wouldn't like it.

" 'Doctor, my mouth has turned into a flower bed. It has tulips.' "

No, Joe . . .

" 'Doctor, you've got to help me. My nose has turned into a frog. I don't know what happened. It used to be a tadpole.' "

He shook his head in disgust. He walked

over to his window and clapped his hands. "Here we go," he said. "Starting all over. The funniest jokes in the world!"

Outside, three young girls were roller-skating. Gary could hear the wheels clacking against the cracks in the sidewalk. He watched them for a while. Two of the girls were much better skaters than the third. The two good skaters kept getting way ahead, then they would turn around and come back for the other one.

"C'mon, Sarah!" he heard one of the good skaters shout.

Sarah fell down. Gary watched her struggle to her feet and go after her friends. He continued to watch until all three girls were out of sight.

He clapped his hands together again. "Okay. Here we go. The funniest jokes in the world.

"I ate a chocolate cookie that was so hard I chipped a tooth. I guess it was a chocolate *chip* cookie."

No, Joe . . .

"I saw a lady wearing sunglasses in the rain. 'Why are you wearing sunglasses in the rain?' 'I don't have an umbrella.' "

In his mind he saw Joe standing there, hands on hips, shaking his head.

"I saw a duck carrying an umbrella. No. No ducks. We already decided that.

"A man goes into a doctor's office. 'Doctor, you've got to help me!' 'What seems to be the problem?' 'It's my green hair.' 'Have you tried dyeing it?' 'I did. I dyed it green.' "

He thought he saw Joe smile.

" 'Why'd you dye your hair green?' 'It's my favorite color.' 'Then what's the problem?' 'I'm going bald.'

Joe shook his head.

" 'Doctor, you've got to help me!' 'What seems to be the problem?' 'I've grown a mustache.' 'So? A lot of people have mustaches.' 'But I'm only twelve years old.' 'Some people mature faster than others.' 'But I'm a girl.' 'A lot of women have facial hair.' 'But I'm also bald.' 'So? There are many beautiful women who have mustaches and are bald.' 'My head gets cold, and it makes me sneeze, and the snot gets caught in my mustache.' "

Joe made a face.

Gary sighed. He glanced at the book on his desk.

" 'How many knees do you have?' 'Three. My right knee. My left knee. And my kidney.' "

For a moment he thought that one was funny, except he remembered he actually had two kidneys, so he'd have to say he had four knees and that just didn't seem as funny as three.

" 'Doctor, you've got to help me! My elbow keeps coming untied. . . . My belly button is out of order. . . . I can't open my chest. . . . I'm losing the leaves in my palm. . . . Somebody threw my waist in the trash. . . . My foot is only eleven inches. . . . I've lost the air in. . . .' "

His thoughts were interrupted by the shrill sound of a vacuum cleaner. He put his hands over his ears and tried his best to ignore it.

"I was walking down the street today and I saw a man with a duck on his head.

"No. No ducks!

"But it wasn't a duck! The man was really a creature from outer space! See, they all look like they have ducks on their heads. In fact, you want to know what they call a man from outer space who doesn't have a duck on his head? Bald."

The noise from the vacuum got louder. Gary slammed open his bedroom door, then glared at his father vacuuming the hall. "Can you do that later?" he shouted over the noise. "I can't concentrate!"

"I'll be done in a minute," said his father.

Gary stepped back into his room and shut the door. "How am I supposed to make up jokes with that thing going all the time?" He looked at the posters on his wall. "Robin Williams doesn't have to listen to a vacuum cleaner when he's trying to make up jokes.

"Maybe I should have played football."

The noise from the vacuum cleaner quieted down as Gary's father moved from the hall-way into the master bedroom, but Gary could still hear it. "Okay, where was I? Ducks. No. No ducks!

"Have you ever tried to brush your teeth with peanut butter?"

If he tried real hard, he could still hear the vacuum cleaner.

He didn't make up any jokes the next day. He had to prepare his book report, and after that he just didn't feel like it.

None of his jokes seemed funny anymore. He tried to remember some of the best jokes he'd made up over the last two weeks, and there wasn't one that was really funny. There were none that would make Joe laugh.

"No wonder everyone thinks I'm a goon," he said.

Friday morning he presented his report on

the book about the pirate and the beautiful maiden. It wasn't that hard. He simply finished reading the book, then told what happened in it.

"Very good, Gary!" Mrs. Carlisle said when he was finished. "I must say, I was pleasantly surprised."

Gary was surprised too. In the old days he would have tried to think of a funny way to tell about the book, maybe even dress up like a pirate—or more like it, dress up like the beautiful maiden with a wig and a dress.

And why? Mrs. Carlisle wouldn't have appreciated it. The kids in the class would have made fun of him. But he would have done it anyway. Why? "Because I'm a goon."

He walked out of class shaking his head. "The funniest person in the world?" he asked out loud. "I'm probably the least funniest person in the world!"

"You've got the funniest butt in the world," said Ryan Utt, who happened to pass by at that moment.

At lunch Joe Reed was hanging out with some eighth-graders, including Philip Korbin, the eighth-grade president who had forced Gary to eat the dirt-covered ice cream bar.

Gary walked right up to them. "Hi, Joe," he said.

Joe turned and looked at him, then smiled. "What it is, Goon," he said.

"Uh . . ." said Gary. He wasn't sure what to say, or if he was supposed to say anything. If Joe had asked, "What is it?" then that definitely would have been a question. But *"What it is"*—Gary didn't know if Joe was asking him a question or not.

"Hey, Goon! Want some ice cream?" asked one of the eighth-graders. Then they all laughed.

Gary shrugged. He was used to kids making fun of him but wished they wouldn't do it in front of Joe.

Joe didn't seem to notice. "Ice cream sounds pretty good," Joe said. "I think I'll get some."

"I'll get it for you," Gary offered.

"Oh, that's o—" Joe started to say.

"What kind do you want?" Gary asked.

"Uh . . . ice cream sandwich," said Joe. "Thanks, Goon." He looked at the other boys and smiled.

"What is he, your dog?" asked Philip.

Gary headed to the vending machines. "Go

fetch, Goon!" Philip called after him, but he pretended not to hear.

As he walked to the vending machine it suddenly hit him that he didn't have any money. He kept going anyway—he didn't know what else to do. He stepped up to the machine and reached into his pocket, but the pocket was empty, like he knew it would be. He tried the coin return. No luck. He pushed the button on the machine, hoping just this once it would work without money.

He stayed away from Joe the rest of the lunch period, and tried his best to avoid him as much as possible during gym.

Joe, for his part, didn't say anything about it.

Friday night was supposed to be his last night to make up jokes. Then he would have a week to put it all together and rehearse before the talent show. He lay on his bed and stared at the ceiling.

"Maybe I should just quit the stupid talent show. Maybe I *should* collect baseball cards."

There was a knock on his door. Then his mother hesitantly entered his room.

He glared at her.

"I know I'm not supposed to disturb you," she said, "but your father and I were thinking about going to a movie, and we thought maybe you'd like to come."

He sighed. "I have to work on my act," he said. "The talent show is less than a week away!"

"We thought you might like to take a break for one night."

"Fine! Okay, I'll take a break! Is that what you want? I'll quit the talent show! Are you happy now?"

"You don't have to snap at me. We thought you might like to go to a movie, that's all. If you don't want to—"

"Fine! I said I'd go. If that's what you want. Let's go to a movie!"

"I just—"

"I said I'd go. What are you waiting for? Let's just go!"

They ended up not going.

16.

Melissa Turbone was wearing a small round hat with straight sides and no brim. It was made out of fake leopard skin.

"It's my brand-new leopard-skin pill-box hat!" she said, then laughed.

Gary didn't get it.

It turned out that there was an old song called "Leopard-Skin Pill-Box Hat." Melissa did a little dance as she sang it for him, using her croquet mallet as a microphone.

"Well, I see you got your
  brand-new leopard-skin pill-box hat!
Yes, I see you got your

brand-new leopard-skin pill-box hat!
Well, you must tell me, baby,
  how your head feels under somethin' like
    that.
Under your brand-new leopard-skin pill-box
  hat!''

Abel stared at her. "Is that the whole song?" he asked.

Melissa shrugged. "One verse anyway."

"Not much to it, is there?" asked Gary.

"I thought it was great!" said Angeline.

"It was written by Bob Dylan," said Melissa, "one of the greatest songwriters to ever live."

Gary and Abel looked at each other. They didn't see what was so great about it. But they had liked watching Mr. Bone dance. She hadn't danced like that when she was Gary's fifth-grade teacher.

Gary was wearing a hat too, a black fedora with a green band.

"So, are you all prepared for the talent show?" asked Melissa.

She suddenly became his fifth-grade teacher again, asking if he'd done his homework.

"It's getting there," he said, trying to sound confident. He couldn't tell her he was thinking of quitting. When she was his teacher, she was always getting down on him for not finishing what he started.

"Look, are we going to sing and dance, or are we going to play croquet?" complained Gus. For once, Gus was winning.

It was Gary's turn. He stepped up and smacked the ball cleanly through the wicket.

Except he hit the wrong ball.

"That was my ball," said Abel. "I'm orange."

"Huh?"

"You're green," said Abel. "You hit the orange ball."

Melissa took off Abel's and Gary's hats, and she put Gary's hat on Abel's head and Abel's hat on Gary's head. "There, all fixed," she said.

Angeline laughed. "You're pretty funny when you're not being a teacher," she said.

"Thank you. I guess," said Melissa. "What's the matter, Gary?" she asked. "You seem a little lost."

"I guess you got your mind on the talent show," said Abel. "Less than a week away."

Gary shrugged.

"You want to know how I keep from getting nervous?" Angeline said.

"How?" asked Gary, although he couldn't imagine Angeline ever being nervous about anything.

"The contest is Friday, right?" said Angeline. "On Saturday it will all be over—*forever*. So don't think about Friday. Think about Saturday."

"Yeah, yeah," said Gus. "That's real good advice, Angelini. But now, Gary. Do you want to know the surefire way to keep from getting nervous on stage?"

"What?" asked Gary.

"Okay. When you get up on stage and look out over the audience, just imagine everyone naked."

"Gus!" exclaimed Melissa as Gary and Angeline laughed.

"What's wrong?" asked Gus. "It's an old trick used by lots of public speakers."

"Well, for one thing," said Melissa, "*I'm* going to be in the audience."

Gary turned bright red. "You're going to be in the audience?" he asked, without looking at her.

"We all will," Abel said. "We wouldn't miss it for the world."

"We'll be your sycophants," said Melissa.

"My what?"

"We'll laugh at every one of your jokes," she explained.

"What if they're not funny?" asked Gary.

"We'll laugh anyway," said Melissa. "Comedians always have friends in the audience to laugh at their jokes. In fact, some comedians actually pay people money to sit in the audience and laugh."

"Isn't that cheating?" Angeline asked.

"No," said Abel. "Sometimes people feel weird about laughing. They have to wait until they hear somebody else laugh, before they think it's okay to laugh. So you get a few people in the audience to laugh every time you tell a joke, and then pretty soon the whole audience is laughing."

Gus burst out laughing.

"What's so funny?" asked Angeline.

"Nothing. Just practicing."

They all practiced their laughs, from mild titters to loud roars. They hooted and howled, wiped their eyes and slapped their knees. Angeline joined in too, even though she wouldn't get to be a part of it.

"I just have one question," said Gus.

"What?" asked Abel.

"How do we know when Gary's told a joke?"

Gary looked up at the sky.

Melissa punched Gus's arm.

"Dog ears!" exclaimed Angeline. "I wish I could be there!"

"I'm sorry, Angelini," said her father. "But the only other flight is in the morning. You'd miss a day of school. And they'd have to make a special trip to take you to the airport."

"Gary's comedy debut is a lot more important than a day of school!"

"Your government sponsors don't quite see it that way," Abel said. "And they're the ones paying for your education. And airfare."

"Dog ears!" griped Angeline.

"I'll be coming right from the talent show to the airport," said her father. "I'll be able to tell you all about it."

Angeline scowled. Then her eyes lit up. "I know," she said. "You and Mr. Bone can get married! They'd have to let me come home for my father's wedding."

Both Abel and Melissa turned red. Each muttered something incomprehensible.

"That's a great idea!" said Gus, slapping Abel on the back.

"Uh, dub, um," said Abel. He cleared his throat.

"I have a more *practical* idea," said Melissa.

"I can borrow my school's video camera. I'll videotape Gary's act for you, Angeline."

"But if you're laughing at Gary's jokes, you won't be able to operate the video camera," said Angeline.

"I'll bring one of my students to operate it. They're better at it than me anyway." She turned to Gary. "You don't mind being videotaped, do you?"

Gary shrugged. "Sure, no problem," he said.

He could see it now: *Goon—The Video!*

17.

He quit the talent show.

"Are you sure you want to do this?" asked Miss Langley.

He nodded, then watched her cross his name off the list.

It was just as well, he thought as he walked across the schoolyard. Now he'd be able to play football after school, or do his homework, instead of wasting so much time making up jokes that weren't funny. And the best part was that he'd still get a hundred dollars from his parents for *not* telling a joke!

"Hey, Ira!" he called. "Michael! Steve!"

Michael and Steve were together, so it didn't

matter that Gary didn't know who was Michael and who was Steve. They both said "Hi, Goon" back to him.

"I'm going to start collecting baseball cards," Gary told them.

All three seemed genuinely gladdened by the news. They told Gary which brand to get, how much they cost, and which store seemed to have the best cards.

"But I guess it doesn't matter with Goon," said Steve (or Michael), "since he doesn't have *any* yet."

For some reason they all thought that was hilarious.

"Can't get any doubles, can he?" asked Ira.

They laughed again.

Gary laughed with them.

The place that Ira said had the best baseball cards happened to be next door to Gary's favorite thrift store. He went into the thrift store first, for old times' sake.

"You're the young man who collects hats," said the elderly woman who ran the store.

He recognized her too. He always figured she didn't have much money, to work in such a place, but there was something about her that impressed him as elegant. She had a very dignified way of talking. And the way she stood, so straight and tall—at least she seemed tall, though if he stood next to her, she'd probably only come up to his chin.

"I collect baseball cards, too," he told her.

"I'm sorry I can't be of help there," she said. "But let me show you something that came in yesterday. I thought of you the moment I saw it."

It was a navy-blue felt homburg, trimmed with a silver ribbon and ornamental button. The feather was yellow with a trace of white around the edges.

Gary tried it on. It was a little too tight for him. He looked at himself in the mirror.

The woman stood behind him. "Very dashing," she said.

It did look pretty good, but he only had enough money for baseball cards. Besides, it was too tight. "Maybe another time," he said.

He went next door and asked for a deck of baseball cards.

At dinner Gary broke the news about the talent show to his parents. "I know you don't like me quitting something in the middle . . ." he started to explain.

"I think you made the right decision," said

his father. "If you must know, we were worried that you might be taking the talent show a bit too seriously."

"We didn't want to see you hurt when you didn't win," said his mother.

He told them about his new hobby—collecting baseball cards.

They approved.

"I used to have quite a baseball card collection myself," his father said. "Willie Mays, Mickey Mantle . . ." He shook his head. "I wish I knew what happened to it. You know what those things are worth these days?" He looked Gary in the eye and spoke very seriously, like he was imparting great fatherly advice. "Whatever you do," he said, "don't throw away your baseball card collection."

Gary promised he wouldn't.

After dinner he tore down his posters of famous comedians. Then he went through his baseball cards and memorized the players' lifetime batting averages.

18.

Gary showed his baseball cards to Ira. They made a trade. Gary traded away two of his cards, and in return got five of Ira's. He wasn't sure why he got five cards when he had to give Ira only two, but he wasn't going to complain.

"I'm just helping a friend get started," Ira explained. "When you're first starting out, the important thing is to get a lot of cards. It doesn't matter who they are."

It all happened so fast Gary didn't understand any of it. Still, he knew he must have done something right, because after Ira told Steve and Michael about the trade, they both wanted to make trades with Gary too.

"Goon, next time you get some new baseball cards," said Michael (or Steve), you come to me first, okay? I'll make you a *good* trade."

"No, come to me," said Steve (or Michael).

"I'm your friend, Gary," said Ira. "I've always treated you right."

Joe let him go out for several passes in gym class, and he caught two of the three Joe threw to him. On one of the passes, Zack told him he made a good catch.

"Zack," said Joe. "You want to play electric football after school?"

Zack shrugged. "I guess."

Gary couldn't imagine why anyone would want an electric football. How would you plug it in? It would have to be battery-operated, or else you'd need a real long cord.

"How about you, Goon?" asked Joe.

"Huh?"

"You want to come over after school and play electric football?"

"Sounds cool," said Gary, trying to sound cool.

He didn't know where Joe lived. He knew he should have just asked him, but for some reason he didn't—like he was afraid to admit he didn't know where Joe lived. It was stupid. He knew it was stupid as he sat at his desk in history, his last class of the day.

He'd have to try to find Joe after school and ask him. Then Joe would wonder why he hadn't asked him earlier. He shook his head and sighed. Or else he could look in a phone book, but there were probably lots of Reeds in the phone book, and phone books didn't always give addresses.

"This is even worse than not bringing him the ice cream sandwich," he said.

When the bell rang, he hurried out of the room, then searched the halls for Joe or Zack. There were four main hallways in the school. He quickly moved from one to the other, and back again. The hallways were crowded at first, and he had to push his way past people to try and see everyone. "Hey, watch it, Goon!" someone yelled at him. But as he continued his search he kept seeing fewer and fewer people in each hallway, until at last hardly anyone was left at all. Dejected, he headed out of the building.

He was halfway home when he suddenly saw Matt, Ryan, and Paul, a block away. He ran to them. "Do you know where Joe lives?" he asked, catching his breath.

"What do you want, Goon?" asked Matt.

He had just told them. "Do you know where Joe Reed lives?" he asked again. "Joe invited me to his house," he added with a touch of pride.

The three boys looked at one another. "I'm not sure of the exact address," said Paul. "It's on Garnet Lane—a two-story blue and white house. There's a weeping willow tree out in front."

Gary didn't ask why the willow tree was crying. *Did its leaves leave?*

"Wait. Where's Garnet Lane?" he asked.

"Do you know where Mica Road is?" asked Paul.

He nodded.

"Just take Mica Road all the way to the end," said Paul. "You can't miss it."

"If you get lost, follow your butt," said Ryan Utt.

Mica Road was a winding road. As Gary rounded each curve he kept hoping he'd see the end, but it just kept winding around.

Maybe the road never ended. He wasn't

stupid. He knew Paul might have made the whole thing up—as a joke. But he felt he was sort of friends with Paul, Matt, and Ryan now. He had played football with them after school. And he had told them he was invited to Joe's. They wouldn't play a joke on Joe.

He kept walking. "Besides, what's so funny about giving somebody wrong directions?" he asked. "There's nothing funny about that."

As he rounded another curve he saw what looked like the end of the road. He walked quickly and soon saw the sign for Garnet Lane.

Garnet Lane was a narrow, quiet street with no sidewalks. He immediately spotted the two-story blue and white house. It really wasn't such a long walk after all.

"What are you crying about?" he asked the weeping willow tree.

No one said he couldn't tell a joke to a tree.

He rang the doorbell.

A woman opened the door. He told her he was there to see Joe.

"My husband?" asked the woman. "He's at his office."

Julie Rose appeared behind her mother. "What's *he* doing here?" she asked.

Gary left.

It wasn't funny. "What's so funny about giving someone directions to Julie Rose's house?"

What bothered him the most was that they thought it would be funny. The reason they thought it would be funny was because Julie was one of the most popular girls in school, while he was . . . well, it showed what they thought he was.

19.

"You get any new cards, Goon?" asked Steve (or maybe Michael).

"Um, no," said Gary. "I haven't had time."

"Time?" asked Michael (or Steve). "How much *time* does it take to buy baseball cards?"

"Gee. It takes a whole two minutes," said Ira.

Ira and the Higgins twins laughed.

"Two and a half minutes if you have to wait for change," said Michael (or Steve).

They all laughed again.

"Two minutes and forty-five seconds if he only has pennies!" exclaimed the other Higgins brother.

Ira laughed so hard he almost fell down.

Gary smiled and shrugged. He had no idea what was supposed to be so funny. Surely they knew it took almost half an hour to get to the store.

"Two minutes and forty-six seconds if he drops one!" said Ira.

They were hysterical.

He leaned against the school building. He saw Joe, but Joe didn't see him. He wasn't sure what he'd say to him—maybe make up something about having to clean the garage.

He felt a hand on his shoulder. "So, Goon," said Matt. "How's Julie?"

Paul and Ryan laughed.

"I guess I should have told you to bring flowers," said Paul. They laughed again.

Ryan nudged Gary with his elbow. "Did you kiss her?"

"No!" said Gary.

"Oh, man, why not?" asked Matt. "That was your big chance."

"Julie's really hot for you," said Paul. "That's why I gave you her address. I knew you'd be too shy to go on your own."

"Yeah, right," said Gary.

Paul looked offended. "I wouldn't lie to you, Goon," he said. "I was just trying to help a friend, but if you're going to be that way about it . . ." He walked away. Matt and Ryan followed.

Gary glanced at a poster for the talent show.

> **CAN YOU SING? DANCE?**
> **OR PLAY THE TUBA?**
> **FLOYD HICKS WANTS YOU!**
> **—IN THE TALENT SHOW**

Two days away. He'd still go to it—but as a spectator. He wanted to hear Joe's rap.

"Wait, let me get this straight, Goon," Joe said in gym. "*You* went to Julie Rose's house!"

Gary shrugged.

Joe and Zack cracked up.

They played flag football.

"I was wide open!" Gary said, returning to the huddle.

"I didn't see you, Goon," said Joe. Then he laughed. "Sorry, but I just keep picturing you at Julie's house." He laughed again. "You have to admit that's funny!"

Gary smiled.

He went straight home after school. He wanted to get an early start on his homework because there was a television show on at eight o'clock that Joe always watched.

He sat at his desk. He thought about the talent show. It was hard for him to believe that he once actually thought he'd be up on stage in front of the whole school telling jokes. Now he couldn't even imagine it.

Two days away. "I'd probably be going crazy right now," he said.

He had to read a chapter in history, but as he stared at the pages he found himself reading the same paragraph over again. He read it at least three times but still didn't know what it said.

"Can't concentrate, huh?" asked a voice behind him.

He turned around.

An old woman was sitting cross-legged on his bed. She was eating mashed potatoes and gravy.

He watched her dig her spoon into the potatoes, then slurp noisily from it. She wore green flannel pajamas and a black bolero, which was the kind of hat worn by Zorro.

"You want some?" she offered, holding out a spoonful of mashed potatoes and gravy.

"Uh . . ." He shook his head. Suddenly he knew who she was. "You're . . ."

"Mrs. Snitzberry," she said with a certain amount of pride. "But my friends call me Gladys."

"Gladys?" asked Gary.

"I said my *friends*," said Mrs. Snitzberry. "You're no friend of mine. What's the big idea?"

"Huh?" he asked.

"Huh?" she repeated.

"What do you mean?" asked Gary.

"What do you mean, what do I mean?" She slammed the plate of potatoes onto the bed. "Quittin' the talent show!"

He shrugged.

"No way, Buster!" said Mrs. Snitzberry. "You've been making fun of me every day for the last two years." She jumped off the bed. "Did I ever complain?" She poked him in the

chest with her finger. "Did I?" She poked him
again. "Did I?"

He backed up against his dresser. "No!" he
shouted. "I didn't even know you were a real
person, or whatever you are."

"Of course I didn't complain," she said.
"Because it was humor! Humor—man's greatest gift! That's what separates humans from all
other animals. That's why they call it humor.
Humans—humor. You never hear dogs telling
jokes, do you?"

"No."

"That's because dogs have no sense of humor!"

As Gary stared at her, her face began to get
blurry and she started to fade, but then
he blinked, and she reappeared as sharp as
ever.

She pulled Gary's ears.

"Ow!" he yelled.

"You can't quit on me now, Buster!" said
Mrs. Snitzberry. "You owe me!"

Gary jerked away. "But my jokes aren't
funny!" he shouted. He sat down on his bed.

"So? That never stopped you before," said
Mrs. Snitzberry.

Gary sighed.

"I was kidding!" said Mrs. Snitzberry. "Boy, you are in sorry shape, aren't you?" She sat down on the bed next to him, right on top of the plate of mashed potatoes and gravy.

"But my jokes aren't funny!" Gary moped. "I did nothing but make up jokes for two weeks—and they all stink! No wonder I never had any friends. I wouldn't be my friend either if I had to listen to me all the time. I've been making a fool out of myself every minute of every day of my whole life."

"So, who hasn't?" asked Mrs. Snitzberry. "Besides, I don't care what anybody says. I think you're hilarious. I've been listening to your jokes. You crack me up."

"Really?"

"Oh, sure, some of them stink." She took her bolero off her head and fanned the foul-smelling air away from her face. "All you have to do is separate the good ones from the stink bombs."

"Which ones didn't stink?" Gary asked eagerly.

"That's for you to figure out," said Gladys. She stood up and walked across the room. Her backside was dripping with potatoes and gravy.

"I guess Rudolph is kind of funny," Gary

said. "I was proud of that one. But it's too late anyway. The talent show is the day after to-morrow. I can't. I wouldn't have any time to put it all together. Or practice. I just can't. Be-sides, I don't even know if Miss Langley would let—"

He turned around with a start as his mother entered his room.

"Are you all right?"

He shrugged. "I'm fine."

"I could hear you shouting all over the house."

"Uh, I was just working on my act for the talent show."

"I thought you quit the talent show."

"I changed my mind."

He jumped as Mrs. Snitzberry pinched his rear end. "All right, kiddo," she said. "Now you're talkin'!"

His mother looked at him oddly. "Are you sure you're all right?" she asked.

"Never felt better!" said Gary. "Besides, quitting never solves anything," he added, trying to sound rational. "You know how you and Dad are always saying that I never follow through on things. Well, this time I'm going to do it. Whatever it takes, one hundred per-cent!"

He-jumped as Mrs. Snitzberry goosed him again.

"O-kay," his mother said with some hesitation. "Just so long as you keep it *in perspective*."

20.

Gary gathered the scraps of paper with all of his jokes and read through them. Maybe they didn't all stink. "In fact, some of them are pretty funny, if I do say so myself." The funny ones were just hard to notice because they were surrounded by garbage.

"What a goon," he muttered as he read one of the more stupid ones.

Rudolph the Red-Nosed Reindeer was funny. He just needed to tighten it up a little bit.

He picked out all the other jokes that fit with Rudolph. He could definitely use the dead skunk jokes.

Kissing worms? Something about it was funny,

but it really didn't make any sense. "No," he decided.

"It's just like life," he philosophized. "I always say whatever comes into my head. And most of it is stupid. So when I say something funny, nobody notices. It's too bad when you're talking to people, you can't go back later and cross out all the stupid things you said."

But that was what was perfect about doing this comedy routine. He could cross out the bad stuff and say only the good stuff. He could say all the funny jokes and none of the stupid ones!

"I should get Abel to help me. Ha. Ha. He could haul all the garbage away in his truck."

He picked out his best jokes and started putting them in some kind of order. It came easy. The good jokes seemed to fit together naturally, almost as if some part of his brain had planned it that way all along. He made up some new jokes without even trying. And the new ones were funnier than some of the old ones.

"No, I can't be sure about that," he said. "Sometimes I think something is funny one day, and then the next day I realize it's stupid. I'll have to look at them again tomorrow and see if I still think they're funny."

Tomorrow? Tomorrow was Thursday!

He just wished he had more time—even one extra day.

He worked all afternoon, quickly ate his dinner, then stayed up until almost midnight. He didn't do his homework. There was just no way.

By the time he went to bed, he knew for the most part which jokes he'd use and the order he'd say them. But it all needed to be polished. He also needed a way to end his routine. He wanted a big finish. "Something to go BANG!" he said as he slammed his fist into his hand.

Plus, he still had to memorize it, get his timing down, and rehearse it. "Of course, first I'll have to hearse," he said. "I mean, I can't *rehearse* until I've at least *hearsed* one time."

He stood up on his bed, pounded his chest like Tarzan, then raised his arms in the air and shouted, "The Goon is back!"

He saw Miss Langley first thing Thursday morning and told her he wanted to be back in the talent show.

"Gary, you can't keep quitting and then signing up, then quitting again," she said.

"I'm in it," Gary said. "I'm not going to quit."

"Well, you'll have to talk to Brenda Thompson. It may be too late."

He found Brenda as she was coming up the stairs along with Julie Rose.

It took Brenda a while to figure out what Gary was talking about because she didn't know he'd ever quit the show.

"So then I'm in?" asked Gary.

"Yes. You were never out," said Brenda.

Julie Rose stared oddly at him. He wondered what Matt or Paul told her about why he had come to her house the other day. Well, he couldn't worry about it. He was back in the talent show—that was the most important thing.

"You gonna stick around for some football?" asked Joe.

Gary sighed. "I can't."

"What's with you anyway, Goon?" Zack asked.

"I have to work on my act for the talent show. It's tomorrow night."

Joe and Zack looked uneasily at each other.

"C'mon, Goon, we really need you," said Joe.

"I thought you were going to do a rap," Gary said.

"I am," said Joe. "I made it up last week. It took about twenty minutes. No big deal. It's just a stupid talent show."

"Yeah, I know," said Gary.

"So what do you say?" asked Joe.

"No, I really need to go home," Gary said. "I guess things don't come as easy for me as they do for you."

"Personally, Goon, I think you need a change in attitude," said Joe. "Lighten up. It's supposed to be fun. Who knows? Anything can happen. Do you hear what I'm saying? *Anything* can happen."

"I know that," said Gary.

"So how about it?" asked Zack. "Are you going to play football or not?"

"I can't."

"Suit yourself," said Joe. "But don't say we didn't warn you."

He tried not to think about it. He remembered what Angeline had said: "Don't think about Friday. Think about Saturday."

"No matter what happens, by Saturday it will all be over—*forever*."

21.

"How could I think that was funny?" Gary asked as he went over his routine. He shook his head in disbelief.

The jokes he used to think were great now didn't seem funny at all. Especially the ones he had made up yesterday.

He decided two of the new jokes were kind of funny. He threw away the other three.

"A bad joke is like a rotten fish," he decided. "You don't know it's bad until the next day when it starts to stink."

He laughed. "That's good! That's funny! I don't think I can use it for my routine, but it's still funny!"

Suddenly, out of nowhere, he remembered one of the other jokes that he had decided not to use. It *was* funny. "Why didn't I think it was funny yesterday?" He wondered what made him suddenly remember it. For that matter, he wondered how he ever thought up any of his jokes in the first place.

BANG! Gary flung himself on his bed, as if a bomb had just exploded in his room—or in his head. He rolled over, looked up at the ceiling, and whispered "Perfect."

He had come up with the big finish for his act.

There was just one question: Would he really have the guts to do it?

"Sure. Why not?"

It meant he'd have to reorganize his whole routine to make the ending work just right. He'd have to change the beginning and the middle to fit the ending, and have the whole thing memorized by tomorrow night.

He hoped the thrift store still had the hat. If not, he could always use one of his other hats, but the one at the thrift store was better because it was a little too tight.

He'd need help, too. His parents wouldn't

help him, that was for sure. He didn't dare tell his parents.

Before he changed his mind, he went to the kitchen and called Gus on the telephone.

Then he called the thrift store and told the woman to save the hat for him. He'd pick it up tomorrow on the way home from school.

Gary went through his routine, from beginning to end, for the third time. It was still too choppy. It needed to be smoother. The timing was all wrong.

He set his notes aside and tried doing it from memory. He was surprised by how much he had memorized. He only had to look at his notes a couple of times.

Then he went through it again, and this time he didn't have to look at his notes at all. He sighed in disgust. "It sounds like I'm reciting the Gettysburg Address or something."

He didn't want it to sound like he was reciting something he had memorized. It had to sound natural, like he was making it up as he went along.

"Okay, one more time."

Timing was the most important thing. He didn't want to pause too long, or too short.

The pause had to be perfect. The pause was all-important.

Or was it? Should he pause at all? When? How long? Why?

"AAAAAAHHHHHH!" he shouted.

He stared at his blank walls. He didn't know. He just didn't know. He had gone over the jokes so many times he didn't even know what was a joke and what wasn't.

There was a knock on his door.

"What!" he shouted.

His mother peeked around the door. "I know you said you didn't want to be disturbed for *anything* . . ."

He glared at her. Actually, he was grateful for the interruption, but he didn't let on.

"Angeline's on the phone," his mother said. "She said it was urgent. Do you want me to tell her you'll call her back?"

"No, I'll talk to her," said Gary.

Gary's mother seemed a little insulted that while she, his own mother, wasn't allowed to interrupt him, he was perfectly willing to leave his room to talk to Angeline.

He took the call in the kitchen. Maybe Angeline'd get to come to the talent show after all.

"Hi. What's up?"

Angeline came straight to the point. "Don't do your act in the show tomorrow."

"What?"

"Something terrible is going to happen," she said. "A disaster."

"Aw, c'mon," said Gary. "I know my jokes may not be funny, but no one's ever called them a disaster. Ha. Ha."

Angeline didn't laugh. "I'm serious, Gary. I started feeling it right after dinner, and then I started crying and couldn't stop. I can still feel it."

Gary could hear her fighting back tears now.

"Please don't do it," she begged. "Just quit the talent show."

"Why? What's going to happen?"

"I don't know, I don't know," said Angeline. "I've never felt something like this before."

"Are you sure it's bad?" he asked. "If you've never felt anything like it before, then how do you know it will be a disaster?"

"I know," said Angeline. "If you break your leg, you don't need a doctor to tell you you can't walk."

Gary took a breath. "It's all memorized," he said.

They stayed on the line for another minute or so without speaking. Then each said good-bye.

Gary gently hung up the phone. He took a breath and turned to see Mrs. Snitzberry, in her green pajamas, sitting cross-legged on the counter, between the sink and the stove.

"Who was that?" Mrs. Snitzberry asked Gary.

"Angeline," said Gary.

"What'd she want?"

Gary thought a moment. "Nothing," he muttered.

"Who are you talking to?" asked Gary's father.

Startled, Gary turned. He hadn't noticed his father reading the paper at the kitchen counter. He looked back at Mrs. Snitzberry, who slowly faded away before his eyes.

"Nobody," he said.

There was still time to quit. There was always time to quit. Right up to the last minute. He didn't have to tell anyone he was quitting. Just not show up.

"Well, if it's a disaster, then it's a disaster," said Gary as he walked across the schoolyard. "Like Miss Longlegs said, I can't keep signing up and quitting, and signing up and quitting. Besides, I already called Gus.

"If it's a disaster, then it's a disaster," he said again. "There's nothing I can do about it. Besides, *how bad can it be?*"

22.

It was time.

"Do you need to use the bathroom before you go?" asked his mother.

"No, I don't have to use the bathroom!" he snapped. He was twelve years old, and his mother still asked him that.

She smiled at him. "You look very handsome," she said. She sounded surprised.

He had chosen his outfit carefully. White shoes, white pants, navy-blue shirt, red suspenders, and the navy-blue homburg that he'd bought at the thrift store after school.

"The talent show isn't until seven o'clock," said his father. "Don't you want any dinner?"

"All the contestants have to get there early," Gary explained. "We need to go over our entrances, exits, how we want to be introduced, stuff like that."

If he ate any dinner, he'd probably throw up.

"Well . . . see you there," his mother said. Then she kissed him.

"Good luck," said his father.

"Oh, Dad, I wanted to ask you something," said Gary. "If there were three birds sitting on a bench, and I shot one, how many would be left?"

"Two."

"Nope, just one," said Gary, "The dead one. The other two would fly away!" He laughed. "Oh well, I guess I don't get the hundred dollars now." He was still laughing as he walked out the door.

He carried a grocery bag full of the props he'd need for his act. It was rolled up at the top so no one could see inside.

He had lied about having to get to school early. He went to Gus's house.

"Wow, you look great!" Gus said when he opened the door.

Gary shrugged. He wished people would stop saying it like that. It made him wonder if most of the time he looked like a slob or something.

Gus's house reminded Gary of a museum, or more precisely, a storage room in a museum. He looked around with awe at all the objets d'art that Gus had collected over his sixteen years as a garbageman: strange and bizarre lamps, vases, wall hangings, a painting of a dead fish, several road signs, a pirate's head, a stuffed armadillo, a candle shaped like a lizard . . .

"Have I ever showed you my law school diploma?" asked Gus.

"You went to law school?"

"No, Kevin David Lally went to law school."

Hanging next to a velvet painting of a sexy lady and her poodle was the dignified law school diploma of someone named Kevin David Lally.

"I wonder why someone would throw away a law school diploma," said Gary.

Gus shrugged. "Why would anyone throw away such a great picture?"

Gary looked back at the painting of the lady

and the poodle. He wished the poodle would move just a little bit to the left.

"So, you really want to do this?" asked Gus.

Gary nodded. "You haven't told anybody?" he asked.

"Are you kidding? And you better not either."

"I won't," Gary promised. "Don't you even want to know why?"

"I figure I'll find out along with everyone else," said Gus.

Gary took a deep breath.

"You're sure?" asked Gus.

"One hundred percent," said Gary.

Fifty-five minutes later, he was standing outside the door to the school auditorium holding his grocery bag full of props.

"So, are you just going to stand there, or are you going to go inside?" asked Mrs. Snitzberry.

He glanced at her. "Disaster is my middle name," he said, then opened the door.

"Pigbubble is my middle name," said Mrs. Snitzberry.

Gary walked down the aisle between the rows of folding chairs, empty now. Miss

Langley was up on stage, along with the custodian. Miss Langley appeared to be testing the microphone, but apparently it wasn't working, because he couldn't hear her.

He could see two other kids also on stage. Susan Smith was doing some warm-up exercises. Marsha Posey was holding a pair of roller skates. An old piano was off to the left.

Gary walked up the stairs on the side of the stage. There were several kids sitting on benches behind the purple plush curtain. Though the curtain was open, the benches still could not be seen from the auditorium.

Gary sat on a bench behind Julie Rose and Brenda Thompson. He set his paper bag under the bench. A red-haired boy whom Gary didn't know was seated at the other end of the bench.

Gary watched Susan Smith in her black leotard raise one leg above her shoulder.

He stretched out his mouth, wiggled his jaw back and forth, and moved his tongue from side to side and in and out.

The boy with red hair looked at him, and Gary stopped his warm-up exercises. The boy was holding what appeared to be a program. Julie and Brenda also seemed to have programs.

"Where'd you get the program?" he asked the boy beside him.

The boy didn't seem to hear him.

"At the back table," said a girl who had sat down on the bench behind Gary. "You can have mine. I have an extra one."

Gary turned around. The girl had short curly blond hair and wore braces. He recognized her from school, but he didn't know her name.

She blushed. "I took two by accident. Here!" She shoved a program at him, then looked away, as if terribly embarrassed by the whole incident.

"I have to go first!" the red-haired boy complained. "I always have to go first. It's because of my name, I know it!"

"Too bad," said Gary, trying not to let on how glad he was that he wasn't the one who had to go first.

He opened the program to the list of contestants.

1. Fred Furst
Fred will do several bird imitations. He is 11 years old and says he's been interested in birds all his life.

165

2. Connie Lee

Connie will play the guitar and sing. She is 13 and has been playing the guitar for two and a half years.

3. Susan Smith

Susan, age 12, will perform gymnastics. She is hoping to be an Olympic gymnast someday.

4. Joe Reed

Joe, age 12, will sing a rap song of his own composition called "Goin' Insane."

5. Brenda Thompson

Brenda, age 12, will sing "Girls Just Want to Have Fun." Brenda is secretary of the student council and the inspiration behind this event.

6. Matt Hughes

Matt, age 12, will tell some of his favorite jokes. His friends say he's the funniest kid in school.

7. Leslie Ann Cummings

Leslie, age 11, will sing a medley of Cole Porter songs. She says her favorite songs are show tunes and she doesn't much care for modern music.

8. Julie Rose

Julie, age 12, will recite several of her own poems. She is president of the student council. She says she wants to be a poet when she grows up, but adds that she wants to make money too.

9. Marsha N. Posey

Marsha, age 13, will perform several tricks on roller skates. "I just like to skate," says Marsha.

10. Alex Roth

Alex will perform Bach's Inventions Nos. 1 and 8 on the piano. He is 13 years old and has been taking piano lessons since age 5.

Gary turned the page, but there were no more contestants listed. He checked again to make sure he hadn't missed his name. "Where am I?" he shouted.

"In the school auditorium," said the red-haired boy, who apparently was Fred Furst, the bird imitator.

"I'm not listed in the program!"

"Are you sure you're supposed to be in it?" asked the girl with braces.

"Yes!"

"You weren't at rehearsal," said Fred Furst.

"What rehearsal?"

"After lunch today," said the girl. "It wasn't really a rehearsal. We just went over what we would do, how we wanted to be introduced, entrances and exits, stuff like that."

"I didn't know about it," said Gary. "Nobody told me. Brenda!"

Both Julie and Brenda turned around. "What's your problem?" asked Julie.

"I'm not in the program," he told Brenda. "Did you ever tell Miss Langley that I wanted to be back in the talent show?"

"What are you talking about?"

"Remember, I told you I wanted to be back in the show, and you didn't even know I quit? Well, I had quit, and you were supposed to put me back on the list."

Brenda made a face. "Don't blame me for your problems."

He jumped up. "Miss Langley!"

She was talking to the principal, Mrs. Ward, at the other side of the stage. He went over to them and waited for a pause in their conversation, but Mrs. Ward never paused, so he just broke in. "Miss Langley!"

Both of them looked at him.

"My name's not in the program."

Miss Langley seemed to be thinking about something else, but managed to focus her attention on him. "Your name's not in the program because you told me you wanted to quit the show."

"But then I said I wanted back in."

"And I told you to talk to Brenda Thompson."

"I did! But she didn't realize I'd quit, so she didn't do anything to put me back in."

Miss Langley sighed. "Why weren't you at the rehearsal this afternoon?"

"I didn't know about it."

Miss Langley shook her head. "Well, I can't do anything about it now. The programs are all printed. I'm afraid it's too late."

"But—"

I'm sorry, Gary, I've got a million things to do." She resumed her conversation with Mrs. Ward about the opening address Mrs. Ward would be giving.

Gary spotted Joe coming into the auditorium, along with Matt, Ryan, and Paul.

"Joe!" called Gary. He jumped off the stage. "Joe. You got to help me!"

Joe put his hands up. "Whoa," he said. "Get

a grip, Goon." He looked Gary up and down. "Nice uni."

"Huh?"

"He likes your clothes, Goon," said Matt. "Your uniform."

"So what seems to be the problem?" asked Joe.

Gary took a breath, then went through it again. "Okay, I was going to be in the show, right? You know that. That's why I didn't play football. But I told Miss Langley I wanted to quit, but then I told her I wanted to be back in, but she said to talk to Brenda Thompson, so I talked to Brenda, but she didn't even know I ever quit, so she didn't put me back on the list, and now Miss Langley says it's too late."

"Okay, okay," said Joe. "Just chill out. I'll go have a chat with Nancy."

"Nancy?" asked Gary.

"Nancy Langley," said Matt.

Gary returned to his seat next to Fred Furst while Joe talked to Miss Langley.

He couldn't believe this was happening. "Why is it always me?" he asked.

His parents were going to be there, and Abel, Gus, Mr. Bone, and that kid Mr. Bone was bringing to run the video camera. Now what was that kid going to think?

Ryan came up alongside him. "Your butt better be in the show," he said.

Julie turned around and made a face at Ryan. "Every other word you say is 'butt.' "

"So?" asked Ryan. "What's wrong with that?"

Joe returned, thumbs up. "You're in, Goon."

Gary could hardly believe it.

"Nancy didn't mean it was too late for you to be in the show. She just meant it was too late to be in the program."

"I hope he's first," said Fred Furst.

"Sorry, Freddy boy," said Joe. "Last."

"That's okay, *Joey boy*," Fred said snidely.

Miss Langley came by a short while later and asked Gary how he wanted to be introduced.

"Just my name, Gary W. Boone."

"And you're going to tell jokes, right?"

He nodded.

"I hope you don't need any props."

"Got everything right here," he said, kicking his paper bag.

"No special lighting or anything?"

"Nope."

Miss Langley shook her head, then smiled. "Why is it always you?"

He shrugged.

The auditorium filled with people, kids and adults. Every chair was occupied, and people were standing along the back and side walls. Gary and the other contestants waited on benches just off stage.

Miss Langley welcomed everyone to the talent show. "Before I introduce Mrs. Ward, I have an announcement. One of our very talented students has inadvertently been left off the program. The final contestant will be Gary W. Boone."

From the left side of the room, about halfway back, Melissa, Abel, and Gus cheered and whistled loudly.

23.

Everyone spoke together. "I pledge allegiance to the . . ."

"Hey, Goon!" Joe whispered sharply. "Take off your hat!"

Gary pretended not to hear him.

". . . of America and to the republic . . ."

"Take off your hat, Goon!" whispered Matt.

"No!" he whispered back, one hand on his heart, the other on his hat.

". . . one nation, under . . ."

"Show some respect, Goon!" whispered Joe.

"He doesn't have to," said Fred Furst.

". . . with liberty and . . ."

Julie Rose turned around. "Don't you love America?"

"Sure, I love America," said Gary. "I just don't want to take off my hat."

"There's no law saying you have to take off your hat for the Pledge of Allegiance," said Fred Furst. "In fact, you don't have to say the Pledge if you don't want to. What's the matter? Don't you believe in freedom of speech?"

The hat stayed on.

The title of Mrs. Ward's opening address was "Inspiration and the Arts."

"Perspiration and the Farts," whispered Matt Hughes.

Brenda Thompson laughed. "Sounds like the name of a punk rock band," she said.

Gary was too nervous to pay attention to the principal's speech. From what he heard, it had something to do with how she wanted to be a ballerina when she was thirteen years old but was too fat.

". . . so I can understand what these young people are feeling right now," said Mrs. Ward.

There was polite applause. Then Miss Langley returned to the microphone and introduced the first contestant. "Fred Furst."

"Good luck," said Gary.

Mrs. Snitzberry sat down in Fred's seat.

"What are you wishing him luck for?" she asked. "He's your competition." She looked toward center stage and shouted, "I hope you get the hiccups!"

Fred approached the microphone.

"Fred will do bird imitations," said Miss Langley. "I understand you've been interested in birds all your life. Is that right, Fred?"

"Yes," said Fred, but the microphone was too high for anyone to hear.

Miss Langley helped him adjust the mike. He spoke into it. "Yes. Ever since I was a baby. The first word I said was 'bird.' "

Several people in the audience said, "Awww."

Miss Langley stepped away.

Gary could see Fred's knees shake.

"Why do I always have to be first?" Fred asked into the microphone.

A few members of the audience laughed, but most of them obviously didn't get the joke.

Fred took a breath. "For my first impression I will do the North American hoot owl."

Fred had a long neck, which seemed to get even longer when he did his bird imitation. "Whoooo. Whoooo.

"Now I will do a North American hoot owl that has been to school: Whom! Whom!"

There was mild laughter. It would have been funnier, thought Gary, if Fred had paused before the punch line.

"That's an old bird imitator's joke," said Fred.

Fred then did impressions of a magpie, "Twitter-peep, twitter-peep"; a nightingale, "Chirp chirp twitter"; and a puffin, "Whoo-peep, whoo-peep."

The audience politely applauded after each one.

Gary didn't know what the real birds sounded like, so he had no idea if Fred's imitations were good or not. It suddenly occurred to him that probably nobody in the audience knew whether the imitations were accurate. Fred could have been making them up! But why would anyone do that?

"Now I will do the mute swan," said Fred. He stood for several minutes without making a sound.

Gradually the audience began to laugh as they caught on to his joke.

He then made the sounds of the pelican, the petrel, and the oriole.

"For my final impression, I'd like to do the redheaded woodpecker."

He took a deep breath, then laughed exactly like Woody Woodpecker!

Gary cracked up. The audience laughed and applauded too.

Fred returned to the bench all smiles.

"That was great!" exclaimed Gary. "You sounded exactly like Woody Woodpecker!" It struck him that Woody Woodpecker was another famous comedian with a *W*.

"I'm just glad it's over," said Fred. "It's weird to talk into a microphone. You hear yourself talking almost before you say it."

"So, were those other ones real bird sounds?" asked Gary.

Fred smiled. He wasn't telling.

Connie Lee was next. She played the guitar and sang. Gary thought she had pretty black hair, but he didn't know much about music, so he couldn't tell if she was any good. Besides, Fred Furst was talking in his ear almost the entire time.

"I'm glad I was first," Fred said. "Now that it's over. I can just sit back and enjoy the show. This is great. I just feel relaxed and charged up. I don't have to sit here and worry the whole time."

"Like me," said Gary.

"Oh, you'll do great," said Fred.

Gary took a deep breath.

Susan Smith did gymnastics. She set out mats on the floor of the stage, then performed several flips, cartwheels, and splits.

"Oooh, that hurts!" Fred Furst said every time Susan did a split.

"Joe Reed," said Miss Langley.

Joe stood up. He winked at Gary, then swaggered confidently up to the mike.

"Joe will sing a rap song that he wrote himself. It's called 'Going Insane.' "

" 'Goin' Insane,' " said Joe. " 'Goin',' not 'Going.' No *g*."

"Excuse me," said Miss Langley. "How could I have made such a horrible mistake?"

Some of the adults in the audience laughed.

" *'Goin'* Insane,' " said Miss Langley.

Joe took a pair of sunglasses out of his shirt pocket and put them on. He started clapping his hands in rhythm until the whole audience joined in, keeping the beat.

"There's a guy at school, and he thinks he's cool,
he wears pink and yellow shorts.

His toes are clean, but his tongue is green,
  and his nose is covered with warts.
Red! Purple! Blue! Black!
Stay away from my baby, Jack!
Goin' insane. Goin' insane.
Has anybody? Has anybody?
  Has anybody seen my brain?
Goin' insane. Goin' insane.
Has anybody? Has anybody?
  Has anybody seen my brain?
Yaaaaaaaaahhhhhhhhhh!"

"I don't think he's *goin'* insane," Fred whispered. "I think he already *is* insane."

The song had several more verses. After a while the audience stopped clapping along, but Joe continued to rap out the words.

"There's a book I read, by a dude who's dead,
  I can't remember his name.
It's about a girl who lost her pearl,
  and they all say I'm to blame.
Oscar! Grover! Big Bird! Ernie!
  It sure has been a long hard journey!
Goin' insane. Goin' insane.
Has anybody? Has anybody?
  Has anybody seen my brain?"

"Yeah, I think it's in a jar at the Smithsonian," whispered Fred.

"Goin' insane. Goin' insane.
Has anybody? Has anybody?
Has anybody seen my brain?
Yaaaaaaahhhhhhhhhhhhhhh!"

Everyone waited to make sure it was over, and then clapped.

Joe smiled and took off his sunglasses.

"Radical," said Matt as Joe sat down next to him.

"Awesome," said Julie Rose.

"Have you tried looking under the bed?" asked Fred Furst.

Gary took another breath. He tried to focus on his own act, how he was going to begin, his exact words, but he couldn't concentrate. It felt like his brain was bouncing around inside his head.

"Brenda Thompson," announced Miss Langley.

Brenda approached the microphone.

"Brenda is the student council secretary. She

was the one who came up with the idea of having this talent show."

The audience applauded.

"What made you think of a talent show, Brenda?"

"Well, people are always putting down the younger generation. Saying we're all on drugs or something. I just wanted to show the kind of talent and spirit we have here at Floyd Hicks Junior High!"

There was more applause.

Fred stuck his finger down his throat.

Brenda sang a song called "Girls Just Want to Have Fun." The backup music played over the speaker system, while above her, different-colored lights flashed on and off.

It seemed to take forever. Gary wished it would all go quicker. He wanted it to hurry up and be his turn before he forgot everything he was going to say.

"She sounds just like the record," Fred whispered.

Gary didn't know. He'd never heard the song before.

"So I understand your friends say you're the funniest kid in school?" said Miss Langley.

Matt Hughes shrugged.

Gary paid close attention.

"Matt will now tell us some of his favorite jokes."

"Well, they're not my *favorites*," said Matt. "I can't say my *favorites*."

Several people laughed.

"All right, Matt!" shouted Joe.

Suddenly Gary had a terrible fear that somehow Matt had made up some of the same jokes he had. What if he'd thought of Rudolph?

Matt took a piece of paper from his back pocket, but it fell out of his hand onto the floor of the stage. He turned his back to the audience as he bent down to pick it up, then unfolded it and stepped up to the microphone.

"What is it that my dad never wanted, but now that he has it, he doesn't want to lose it? A bald head. What do you call a sleeping bull? A bulldozer. We have a great watchdog. Whenever a booger—I mean burglar. I don't know why I said 'booger.' " He laughed. "I guess I have boogers on the brain!" He looked back down at his paper. "Whenever a burglar comes, he hides under the bed and watches. I'm glad my parents named me Matt, know why? Because that's what everyone calls me."

Gary exhaled. It's a tough crowd tonight, he thought. True, Matt didn't pause, and he lost the flow with all that talk about boogers, but still, those were four pretty good jokes and hardly anyone laughed.

"What'd the judge say when a skunk came to court? 'Odor in the court.' "

Gary's heart jumped a little bit. For a second he was absolutely sure Matt was going to tell some dead skunk jokes.

"If you drop a white scarf into the Red Sea, what will it become? Wet."

Matt continued to tell his jokes. He obviously hadn't made up any of his own—Gary had heard them all before. But that didn't seem to ease Gary's mind. Watching Matt tell jokes, as he himself would soon be doing, just made him feel more nervous.

Matt began another joke. "A man and woman got married and were going on their honeymoon. They were in the hotel room, and they both started taking off their clothes. The man looked at the woman and . . ."

Miss Langley quickly walked to the microphone. "Thank you very much, Matt," she said. "That was very good." She clapped her hands, and the audience joined in the applause.

"I was afraid that might have been one of his *favorites*," Miss Langley explained.

More people laughed at that than at any of Matt's jokes.

"Leslie Ann Cummings," said Miss Langley.

Gary nearly jumped as he felt a hand on his shoulder.

"Wish me luck," said the girl with braces.

He looked back at her and said, "Break a leg."

She smiled.

"Break both legs, tinsel teeth!" said Mrs. Snitzberry, now seated behind Gary in Leslie Ann's seat.

Leslie Ann was wearing a long skirt that almost touched the floor.

"I understand you don't much care for modern music," said Miss Langley.

Leslie Ann shrugged. "I like it okay."

She sang "Anything Goes" by Cole Porter.

"In olden days a glimpse of stocking
was looked on as something shocking . . ."

She raised her skirt just a little bit, revealing a glimpse of her stocking.

"Now heaven knows,
anything goes!"

She twirled and kicked her leg up high, revealing a lot more.

Gary smiled as he watched her. He had always thought he didn't like music, but he liked watching and listening to Leslie Ann. She really seemed to put her heart and soul into it as she belted out the words.

> *"Good authors too, who once knew better*
> *   words,*
> *   now only use four-letter words,*
> *writing prose.*
> *Anything goes!"*

She did one other song, "You're the Top," and then returned to the side of the stage, her face red and glowing.

"That was really good," Gary told her.

"You're sweet," she said.

Julie Rose was not the least bit nervous.

"I understand you want to be a poet but you also want to make money," said Miss Langley.

"Well, I don't want to starve or anything,"

said Julie. "All you ever hear about are starving poets. I'm going to go to law school, and then I want to be on the Supreme Court. But instead of just stating my court decisions, I plan to recite them in verse."

"That would be a refreshing approach," Miss Langley said. "We could probably use a few good poets on the Supreme Court."

Several people applauded.

"Give me a break," murmured Fred Furst.

Julie recited some of her poetry.

Gary understood poetry even less than music. He tried again to focus on his own act. He was afraid he might have practiced too much. Comedy was supposed to be spontaneous.

It wasn't too late to quit. Not really.

The audience clapped loudly for Julie as she returned to her seat.

Gary had heard the expression "a cold sweat," but he had never before realized there actually was such a thing. His hands were sweating, yet felt ice-cold.

"Marsha N. Posey," announced Miss Langley.

Gary looked at his program. It was going

too fast! After Marsha was Alex Roth, then him!

Marsha already had on her roller skates. She skated around in circles, forward and backward. One of the benches had been brought to the center of the stage, and Marsha jumped over it, first forward, then backward.

She approached the end of the bench, jumped on it, then skated on one foot the length of the bench and jumped off, still on one foot. She turned around and skated the length of the bench the other way, this time using her other foot.

"I can't even skate on two feet," said Fred Furst.

"Me neither," said Leslie Ann Cummings, behind him.

"Alex Roth," said Miss Langley.

"Oh, God, I'm next!" Gary moaned.

"Relax," Fred whispered. "Have fun."

That was easy for Fred to say. Fred was done. He was lucky. He got to go first.

The piano was rolled to center stage. Alex played two short pieces by Bach: Invention No. 1 in C Major and Invention No. 8 in F Major. Again, it was music, so Gary didn't know if he played well or not. Alex didn't seem to make any mistakes, but only Bach knew for sure, and he was dead.

Gary took several more deep breaths. It was supposed to help him relax, but instead, it made him lightheaded and dizzy.

"I know it's been a long night," said Miss Langley, "but we have one more talented contestant: Gary W. Boone."

He wet his pants.

24.

Gary held the grocery bag full of props in front of his pants as he made his way to center stage. He had no idea how big a spot he'd made, or if it even showed—though he was wearing white pants, so it probably did—but he wasn't about to drop the bag and look.

"Gary will tell jokes," said Miss Langley.

He heard cheers from Abel, Gus, and Melissa, but he couldn't see them because the bright lights were shining on him, and the audience was in the dark.

"Thank you, Miss Longlegs," he said.

The audience laughed.

"Why, Gary!" said Miss Langley with mock

embarrassment. "I never thought you noticed."

The audience laughed again.

It took him a moment to realize what he had said. "I'm—I'm s-sorry," he stammered. He heard his voice boom over the speaker system. Like Fred Furst had said, it was almost as if he heard his voice coming from the speakers before he even said the words.

He stared out at the audience. His mind froze. He couldn't remember how he was supposed to begin.

"My friends call me Goon," he said, "and you are my friends." He didn't know why he said that. He sounded like a politician, not a comedian. "See, you take the G from Gary and the 'Boone' from 'Goon,' and then—No, wait, did I say 'Boone'? I mean—Okay, let me start over. Well, no, I won't start over—you should never start over. I guess I shouldn't have eaten a dead skunk for breakfast, ha ha."

It was all coming out wrong. He wasn't supposed to say that yet. "And we didn't have any maple syrup, ha ha!"

He heard Abel laugh loudly. Nobody else joined him.

"Reminds me of that rude policeman, Rudolph the—"

At that moment Ryan Utt and Paul Wattenburg rushed the stage. Instinctively, Gary dropped the paper bag, grabbed his hat with both hands, and held it firmly on his head as Paul smashed a cream pie in his face. Ryan sprayed him up and down with a seltzer bottle. Then the two boys disappeared from the stage as quickly as they had come.

There were a few gasps, but mostly everyone just sat in shocked silence. Miss Langley stood up.

With one finger Gary wiped the cream away from his eyes. He spoke into the microphone: "That was my fan club."

Everyone laughed.

He licked his finger, then turned toward Paul and Ryan, who were at the foot of the stage stairs. "My compliments to the chef."

The audience laughed again, and Miss Langley sat back down.

"It happens to me wherever I go," said Gary. "That's why I always carry this!" He reached into his paper bag and pulled out a large bath towel.

The audience laughed as Gary wiped his face with the towel. When he finished, he held it up and said, "Don't leave home without it."

They actually applauded.

The two disasters had canceled each other out. His pants were now wet anyway from the seltzer. He felt calm and in control. The audience was on his side.

"As I was saying, my name is Gary Boone, but all my *friends*"—he glanced at Paul and Ryan—"call me Goon."

They even laughed at that.

"See, my first name's Gary and my last name's Boone, so when you put them together you get Goon. Now, if you think that's bad, I've got a sister named Sally. Everyone calls her Saloon."

There was more laughter, led by Gus, Abel, and Melissa.

"I have another sister named Barbara. You know that we call her?" (Pause: One . . . two . . . three.) "Baboon."

He waited a moment. "Of course, it doesn't help that she is always eating bananas and scratching her armpits.

"But probably the person with the worst name is my best friend, Phil Hart. I can't even tell you what we call him."

He waited as bits of laughter broke out in different sections of the audience as different people got the joke.

"Now, you're probably wondering why I'm wearing this hat. Well, it's kind of a long story."

"Tell us!" shouted Gus.

Gary smiled. "Okay, I will. It started out this morning. I guess you might say I got up on the wrong side of the bed this morning." He paused. "My bed is up against the wall." He paused again. "I think I broke my nose."

Several people laughed.

"I went downstairs, where my mother was making breakfast. I couldn't smell a thing." Another pause. "Actually, that's not bad when my mother is cooking breakfast. I should break my nose more often."

He thought he heard his mother laugh.

"She's not exactly the greatest cook. Last night we had fish for dinner. My mother fed them worms. The rest of us had spaghetti. You know the difference between a plate of spaghetti and a plate of worms? Well, you better find out if you're ever invited to our house for dinner!

"After breakfast I went to the doctor.

" 'Doc, I think my nose is broken.'

"He looked at it and said, 'No, it's still running.'

" 'But Doc,' I said. 'I don't smell.'

193

" 'Oh yes you do,' he said. 'You stink!' "
Gary held his nose with one hand and fanned
away the foul-smelling air with the other, im-
itating the doctor.

The audience laughed, so Gary pretended
they'd hurt his feelings. "Sure, you laugh. Well,
I didn't think it was very funny. I thought he
was being rude. I don't know—maybe it was
my fault. Maybe I shouldn't have eaten two
dead skunks for breakfast."

The audience laughed. He hadn't planned
to say *two* dead skunks, but at that moment it
suddenly seemed funnier than just one.

"It was the only time a doctor has ever told
me *not* to say 'Ahhhhh.'

"So, do you want to know why I ate two
dead skunks for breakfast?"

"Why?" shouted Melissa, Abel, and several
other people near them.

"We were out of waffles," answered Gary.
"But I started to tell you why I'm wearing this
hat. See, the doctor gave me some special
mouthwash and soap." He reached into his
paper sack and pulled out a used bar of soap
and half a bottle of mouthwash. "This stuff is
so strong you can't even buy it without a prescription." He took a whiff of the soap, then
quickly turned his head away and coughed.

"So I went home and gargled. Actually, the mouthwash didn't taste too bad." He looked at the bottle. "Sort of like, um, well, actually it tasted a lot like a dead skunk.

"Except without the maple syrup."

"Oh, gross!" someone shouted, amid the laughter. That just made the crowd laugh more.

For a second Gary stopped and enjoyed the laughter. He felt completely at home on stage, in front of a microphone. Everything was clicking for him. He had his routine down pat, but he was also ad-libbing to give it spontaneity.

"That reminds me. You know how to tell a girl worm from a boy worm? By kissing them."

Everyone laughed.

He hadn't planned to tell that joke. It just felt right at that moment. He quickly went on before anyone realized it made no sense.

"I got in the shower, and put that special soap all over me." He pulled a washcloth out of his sack.

They even laughed at that, which surprised him because he didn't remember thinking that was a joke.

He pretended he was in the shower. He washed his chest, his feet, behind his knees, and under his arms. It all worked better than he'd planned, since he was wet from the seltzer. He smelled his armpit, then washed it again.

"So there I was, all covered with this special soap from head to toe, and suddenly the water shut off! The smelly stuff was even in my hair. And no water! Can you imagine that?

"You can?

"You people are sick! I don't imagine any of you naked in the shower!"

He paused. "Well, maybe some of you." He looked off stage left. "I sometimes like to imagine Miss Longlegs in the shower."

She burst out laughing.

He continued to look at her. "And you always thought I wasn't paying attention in class."

She covered her face with her hands and shook her head.

He looked back at the audience. "So there I was, covered with soap, no water—" He stopped. "You know, I really got this backward. My friend Phil·Hart I told you about— he gave me advice on how to keep from getting stage fright. He said, 'Just imagine everyone in the audience naked.' "

A few people laughed.

"Instead, I've got everyone in the audience imagining me naked!

"Of course, that's Phil's advice for anything. 'You know how to keep from crying at funerals? Imagine everyone naked.' 'You know what to do if you get sent to the principal's office? Imagine the principal naked.' "

He glanced at Mrs. Ward, but she didn't seem to think it was funny.

"Phil was a great baseball player until he played against an all girls' team." The audience was already laughing, anticipating the punch line. "He struck out looking every time.

"So, you want to know why I ate two dead skunks for breakfast?"

"Whyyyy?" at least half the audience shouted back to him.

"I couldn't wait until lunch.

"Okay, so I'm standing in the shower with no water—"

Gary stopped. He picked up his towel and wrapped it around his waist. "There, that's better.

"Do you want to know the real reason I ate two dead skunks for breakfast?"

"Whyyyy?" almost everyone shouted.

"Because one's just never enough. Like po-
tato chips.

"So I'm standing in the shower with the
special soap all over me, with nothing to do
except wait for the water to come back on. It
was miserable. I got to thinking about my rude
doctor. He reminded me of that famous rude
policeman. Officer Ed. You know, the one they
wrote the song about."

He looked at the audience as if surprised they
didn't know what he was talking about. "You
know about Officer Ed, don't you?

"He was always very rude to everyone. Even
more rude than my doctor.

"One day a husband and wife came to a
street corner where Officer Ed was directing
traffic.

" 'Good morning, Officer Ed,' said the husband.

" 'Shut up!' said Officer Ed. 'I suppose you
want me to stop traffic now, just so you and
your ugly wife can cross the street.'

" 'My, it's a beautiful day,' said the wife.

" 'It's going to rain, stupid!' said Officer Ed.
'I've never met such stupid people in all my
life.'

" 'But there's not a cloud in the sky,' said
the woman.

" 'Read my lips, lady,' said Officer Ed. 'It's going to rain.'

"Sure enough, before they even made it across the street, the clouds blew in and the rain poured down. The man and woman had to run under a doorway for cover.

" 'My goodness,' said the woman. 'Officer Ed is extremely rude.'

" 'Yes, dear,' said her husband. 'But he knows rain.'

"Well, it just so happened that the man and woman were songwriters, and that's what gave them the idea for that famous song."

Gary put his hands on his hips and looked at the audience as if surprised they didn't know the song. "Oh, c'mon, you know that song!"

He spoke the title very slowly. "Rude . . . Officer . . . Ed . . . knows . . . rain . . . dear."

Gary repeated the title, this time singing it to the tune of the well-known Christmas song. "Rude Officer Ed knows rain, dear."

There were many groans amid the laughter.

"So, you want to know why I ate two dead skunks for breakfast?"

"Whyyyy?"

"Because the live ones squeal when you stick in the fork."

The towel, which had been wrapped around him, suddenly fell to the floor.

The audience laughed hysterically as he quickly picked it up and wrapped it back around himself, feigning embarrassment.

"I found out later that the reason I had no water was because my dad was fixing something in the other bathroom." (Pause: One . . . two . . . three.) "He was changing a light bulb.

"My dad's great around the house. He turns off the water when he changes a light bulb, and he turns off the electricity when the toilet gets backed up. 'Can't be too careful,' he says."

Gary thought he heard his father laugh.

"He's right too, especially when he's the one doing the work. He recently installed an automatic garage door opener and a new toilet. Now every time you push the button to open the garage, the toilet flushes. And every day when he drives home from work, he honks his horn, and then I run to the bathroom and push the lever down on the toilet so the garage door will open.

"Well anyway, after about two hours, my dad finished changing the light bulb and the water came back on. By the time I got out of the shower, it was time for lunch. You want to know what my mother made for lunch?"

"Whaaaat?"

Gary shrugged. "A peanut butter and jelly sandwich. Why'd you want to know that?

"But I was telling you why I was wearing this hat. See, I had that special prescription soap in my hair for two hours, so . . ."

In one sweeping motion he took off his hat and bowed.

He was bald from his ears up.

The audience went wild.

25.

"That was . . . *something*," said Miss Langley joining Gary at center stage. "May I feel?"

"Sure."

The audience laughed as she ran her fingers over the top of Gary's bald head. "Smooooth," she said.

Gary smiled.

"So why'd you leave the hair on the sides of your head?" she asked.

"That way you couldn't tell I shaved my head when I was wearing my hat," he explained. "See." He put the hat back on his head, then took it off again.

The audience applauded.

His hair formed a halo around his head.

"Clever," said Miss Langley. "So, Gary W. Boone. What does the W stand for?"

"Wolfgang," said Gary.

Everyone laughed again.

"Rocket!" said Fred Furst as Gary, hat on head, returned to the bench behind the curtain.

"C'mon, Goon, take your hat off," said Brenda. "Let us see your head."

Gary obliged. All the other contestants gathered around. Only Joe stayed away.

Paul Wattenburg and Ryan Utt were also backstage.

"No hard feelings, huh, Goon?" said Paul.

"Are you kidding, that was great!" said Gary as Marsha Posey touched his head. "Pie in the face. Seltzer. It was classic!"

Leslie Ann Cummings looked but didn't touch.

"You're all right, Goon," said Paul.

"You really are bald," said Ryan.

"As bald as your butt," said Gary.

All the contestants were brought back on stage. Miss Langley held her hand over each student's head, and the audience applauded accordingly.

Third prize, ice cream sundaes for two, went to Susan Smith, the gymnast. Brenda Thompson won second prize, the gift certificate at Zulu's Records. And to thunderous applause, Gary Wolfgang Boone was awarded first prize.

He tipped his hat to the crowd.

His parents were waiting for him when he stepped down from the stage. "I'm just glad I didn't know," said his mother. Then she hugged him.

His father hugged him as soon as his mother let him go.

"You're not mad?" asked Gary.

"You already cut it off," his mother said. "What good would it do to be mad? Just do me a favor. When we visit Grandma next week—leave your hat on."

"There's the superstar!" said Abel Persopolis. "May I have the privilege of shaking your hand?"

Gary shook Abel's hand, and Gus's. Gus winked at him.

Melissa took off Gary's hat and kissed him right on top of the head.

"You must be Gary's parents," said Abel. "Abel Persopolis. I've been looking forward to meeting you for a long time."

"Spencer Boone," said Gary's father, shaking his hand. "But you can call me Spoon."

They all laughed.

"Too bad Angeline couldn't be here," Gary's mother said.

"Well, we videotaped it for her," said Melissa. She nodded to the boy holding the camcorder. "We'll show it to her tomorrow before the croquet game."

"Oh, that's perfect!" said Gary's father. "And Gary, you be sure to wear your hat until after the video is over. No, even better, take it off right at the same time you take it off in the video!"

"You might want to shave your head again tomorrow morning so there's no stubble," suggested Gary's mother.

Gary looked at them in disbelief. Were these his parents?

"Why don't you all come over for dinner after your croquet game," said Gary's mother. "I've got a new recipe for dead skunk."

Abel, Gus, and Melissa laughed.

"Just be sure to bring a garage door opener

with you," said Gary's father. "In case you have to use the bathroom."

Abel pointed at Gary and said, "Now I know where you get it."

The fifth-grader who had operated the camcorder asked Gary for his autograph.

Fred Furst was leaving with three people who were obviously his parents and big sister.

Gary went after them. "Hey, Fred!"

Fred stopped and turned.

"Thanks," said Gary.

"For what?"

Gary smiled and shrugged. "You want to play croquet tomorrow?"

"Okay."

"Great," said Gary.

He gave him directions to Angeline's house. "Oh, and you have to wear a hat."

"No problem," said Fred.

"And if anybody asks you, 'What's cookin'?' you say 'Mashed potatoes and gravy.' "

"Why?"

Gary shrugged. "I don't know."

"Okay," said Fred.

"Do your bird calls for Angeline. She'll know if you were just making them up."

Fred smiled.

Mrs. Carlisle, Gary's English teacher, firmly shook Gary's hand. "Congratulations," she said. She had a surprisingly strong grip.

"Thanks."

"You put a lot of work into it, didn't you?" she asked.

He nodded.

"It showed," she said. "Now if only you'd put that same creativity and effort into your classwork . . ." She smiled at him.

Gary shrugged. "I'll try," he said, although he knew he wouldn't. Why would he ever want to work that hard for *school?*

"Very professional," Mrs. Carlisle continued. "Have you ever thought about being a stand-up comic?"

"Not really," said Gary.

"Hey, Goon. Football tomorrow?" asked Joe Reed.

Gary turned. "Can't. I'm playing croquet."

"Croquet?" asked Joe. "You crack me up, Goon." He reached toward Gary as if he was going to rub his head, but then he brought his hand back—afraid to touch it.

"You want to play?" asked Gary.

"Croquet? You sure you didn't shave off part of your brain?"

"Mr. Bone will be there. Remember, our fifth-grade teacher? And Angeline Persopolis."

"You're sandbagging me, right?" asked Joe. Gary still didn't know what he meant by that.

Zack joined them. "So, is he going to play?"

"He can't," Joe said somewhat snidely. "He's playing croquet with his fifth-grade teacher."

Someone tapped his shoulder. He turned around.

"Congratulations, Gary," said Leslie Ann Cummings.

"Thanks. I thought you should have won too. You sang better than Brenda Thompson. I would have voted for you."

She smiled. "Oh, I don't care. You know how it is. The popular kids always win. I mean, unless you're *supertalented*."

Gary blushed.

"So, when will it grow back?" she asked.

It took Gary a second to figure out what she meant. "Oh, I don't know. Probably about four months."

"Oh, that's perfect!" said Leslie Ann. "I get my braces off in four months."

She hurried away.

Gary watched her for a moment. Did she just say what he thought she said?

He'd left his bag of props under the bench on stage. He went back up to get it, then sat down for a moment and rested on the bench. He suddenly felt very tired.

He took a long deep breath as he held his chin in his hands, propped up by his elbows. The buzz of the auditorium seemed to surround him, or maybe it was his own brain that was buzzing.

He took another long deep breath.

He looked at the back of the purple curtain. It had worn thin in a number of places and was tattered around the edges. It really was quite dingy.

He would have thought the school would take better care of its curtain. At least clean it once in a while!

He took out his big towel and wiped a tear from his eye.

He was still crying fifteen minutes later when his mother came up on stage to see what had happened to him.

THE CRITICS RAVED:

"Hilarious! Stupendous! Amorphous!"

—Fred Furst

"I never stopped laughing. Funny? He redefined the word. 'Funny' doesn't mean what it meant yesterday."

—Angeline Persopolis

"He deserved to win. He was quite funny, in an amazing sort of way."

—Nancy Langley

"Well, sure. I could have won too if I had shaved my head."

—Matt Hughes

"The world's greatest sandbagger!"

—Joe Reed

"He's going to be famous someday."

—Abel Persopolis

"That's my son. I used to be known as quite a wit myself. Or was that a half-wit? Ha. Ha. He even looks like me. And who knows, maybe in a few years, after I lose a little more hair, he'll look more like me."

—Spencer Boone

"Brilliant! Just don't look at him."

—Prentice Boone

"I laughed. I don't know why I laughed. But I laughed."

—Mrs. Walls

"Yeah, he's hilarious. Now, are we going to play football, or are we just going to stand around talking about Goon?"

—Zack

"I've known Gary since he was in my fifth-grade class. I always knew he had it in him. I was glad to see him finally reach his potential. Yuck, I sound just like a teacher, don't I?"

—Melissa Turbone

"Way to go, Buster! Now, if you'll excuse me, it's time for my mud bath."

—Gladys Pigbubble Snitzberry

"I don't get it."

—Ira Feldman

"He's the tops. He's the Tower of Pisa. He's the smile on the Mona Lisa."

—Leslie Ann Cummings

"He's still a you-know-what."

—Ryan Utt

"*Strange*, but funny. Still, I don't think he should have won *first* prize."

—Brenda Thompson

"I didn't think all the jokes about nudity were appropriate. This is a school, not a Las Vegas nightclub."

—Mrs. Ward

"Like I'm really going to imagine Gary Boone naked. Gross!"

—Julie Rose

"You have to admire the Goon."

—Paul Wattenburg

"How could flushing a toilet cause a garage door to open? That's impossible."

—Michael Higgins

"Don't ask me. I don't know who shaved his head."

—Gus

"He's got something inside him that I don't think any of us realized before. There's a spark."

—Mrs. Carlisle

"So what? It was just a rinky-dink junior high school talent show."

—Philip Korbin

"I swear I don't know Gary Boone, but my teacher read this stupid book to our class and now everyone is picking on me. Thanks a lot, Goon!"

—Phil Hart
(Foxbury, North Dakota)

Louis Sachar is often asked where he gets his ideas for books. "I listen a lot to kids," he says. If what he hears is funny, there is a good chance it will wind up in a book. And judging from his fans, Louis is the author of some of the *funniest* middle-grade books around — including *Sideways Stories from Wayside School* and *There's a Boy in the Girls' Bathroom* (winner of 13 state children's-choice awards).

Louis lives with his wife and daughter in Austin, Texas.